OFFICER DOWN

OFFICER DOWN

◆

A Cockade City Novel

Steve Armstrong

iUniverse, Inc.

New York Lincoln Shanghai

Officer Down
A Cockade City Novel

iUniverse, Inc.

For information address:
iUniverse, Inc.
2021 Pine Lake Road, Suite 100
Lincoln, NE 68512
www.iuniverse.com

ISBN: 0-595-31712-X

Printed in the United States of America

For SGM

Acknowledgments

♦

As with any book, there are several people that I need to thank and several people I'm sure I'm forgetting to thank, but here it goes.

First, I'd like to thank all of the readers who bought the first two Cockade City novels—*Do Not Go Gentle* and *Indecent Liberties*. Without you, there would be no *Officer Down*.

Sincere appreciation goes to Mike Elmore, Al Lee, Morris Jones, Gerald Mann, Carl Moore, and William Rhode for their inspiration, stories, and assistance. Thank you to my editor, Kate Harris and all the folks at iUniverse.

I'd also like to thank Lelia and Ann Taylor from the Creatures 'n Crooks Bookshoppe for their continued support of local authors. It's the smaller, mom and pop (or in this case mom and daughter!) bookstores that have always been more customer-oriented and better able to serve the needs of the reader than any giant chain warehouse store. Please visit them online at www.cncbooks.com.

Finally, I'd like to thank my wife, Anna, for her continued support throughout this process. She has had the unenviable task of keeping me grounded when my head was in the clouds of imagination. For that I will be eternally grateful.

Author's Note

♦

As I write this, 2003 is coming to an end. This year my father, Edward, and I released the first of a new series of American Advisors in Vietnam books, *Covan My*. I must admit that writing a book between books proved to be quite a challenge. My dad experienced a personal tragedy that left him blind and depressed. Through our writing, we were able to bring him out of that depression as we channeled his military experiences into a story of modern warfare. You can check out this book at:

www.vietnam-stories.com

Now, back to the police books. My first two Petersburg Police novels, *Do Not Go Gentle* and *Indecent Liberties,* were both local bestsellers and generally well received. I've always said that the best compliment I've gotten has been from folks who don't read that much, but say they liked my books. I know a lot of police officers and family and friends of police officers in particular who liked the books, especially those from the Richmond/Tri-City area. But I hope that, if nothing else, I've told a good story.

That brings us to this book. Again, although some of the scenarios, characters and situations may seem familiar, this is a work of fiction. This is not a documentary re-telling of any specific incident or occurrence. Please keep this in mind if, as you're reading, you come across a guy who you're just sure is someone you know—it's not.

Now, let's hit the streets!

—Steve Armstrong
December, 2003

*"Everybody knows that the world is full of stupid people,
so meet me at the mission at midnight, we'll divvy up there.
Everybody knows that the world is full of stupid people,
I've got the pistol, so I'll keep the pesos-
yeah, that seems fair."*

—The Refreshments, "Banditos"

PROLOGUE—PART ONE

♦

January 14, 0004 Hours

Officer Joe Buckley, veteran patrolman of the Petersburg Bureau of Police, blinked rapidly as he stared down the barrel of his own gun. It had happened so quickly that he couldn't believe that he was now facing every cop's worst nightmare.

"Look, man..." Joe stammered, trying to be calm. Joe was on the Bureau's famed Crisis Response Team, or C.R.T., as a negotiator. He was trained to negotiate with criminals in high-tension situations. They say that in an emergency, one reverts back to their training. Joe did all he could do—negotiate. For his life. "Don't do this...I know it looks bad, but you don't have to do this. If you just-"

"Shut the fuck up, man!" The man now holding Joe's weapon-and pointing it directly at Joe's chest-was scared. Joe could see it in his eyes. "Man" was really stretching it. *Kid* was more like it. Maybe no more than seventeen or eighteen, tall and skinny. The kid's hands were shaking. The gun-Joe's gun-was shaking in them. "Just shut the fuck up!"

It had all gone so bad so quickly. Joe had responded to the 1900 block of Commerce Street on a disturbance call. Neighbor lady had called the police and said a group of kids were breaking into parked cars. Happened all the time. Most of the people who actually lived in the neighborhood just left their car doors unlocked and took their valuables inside at night.

Joe Buckley and Senior Police Officer Lee Kole had been sent on the call. It was a little after midnight on their 11 p.m.–7 a.m. shift. Joe had arrived first. He killed his headlights about three blocks before-to help him sneak up on the kids-but as he slid down the busy street, he could hear the shouts. He had been spotted.

"Five-Oh! Five-Oh!" The pre-teen lookouts called out. It made Joe smile to know that these kids were still using a reference to an old T.V. show that was canceled long before they were even born.

Joe gunned the engine of his Police Package Ford Crown Victoria and hit the lights. All of them: headlights, blue lights, takedowns and alley. He grabbed for his radio mic.

"103," he gave his unit number to police dispatch.

"103, go ahead," came the disembodied voice of the communications operator.

"103, mark me 10-6. Be advised that I've got about five or six 10-97's running now, upon my arrival."

"10-4, 103," the dispatcher answered. "112?" She called out to Kole.

"112 direct to 103, I'm coming to you from headquarters, you need me to go code three?" Styles asked Joe if he should respond as fast as he could with blue lights and sirens.

"That's a negative, 112. They're in the wind. I'm gonna canvass the area, check for any broken windows."

"10-4," Kole said, the roaring of his engine audible thorough the background noise.

Joe parked his marked patrol car at an angle in the middle of the street and clicked on the rear flashers. He stepped out and looked around. Nothing. He took a deep breath of the crisp January air and zipped up his jacket. Taking out a pack of his favorite brand of cigarettes (whatever was the cheapest), Joe lit one and walked along the parked cars, taking in the scenery.

Commerce Street was anything but a scenic route. At one time, with several major businesses along this stretch of road, Commerce Street was home to both industry and trade. Now, the only trade came in little plastic bags, dispensed by not-so-friendly neighborhood corner dealers.

Joe took a long drag on his cigarette and exhaled. He had his flashlight trained on the windows of the parked cars and noticed the shards of shiny safety glass on the ground next to a late model Honda. Using his flashlight to scan ahead, he saw more broken glass, and then he saw-well, he wasn't sure what it was. It looked like feet. Hanging out of an old, beat up Lincoln. He walked closer to the feet.

When he got right up on the feet, he saw that they were attached to a young man wearing headphones. Joe could hear the melodious sounds of hardcore rap coming out the tiny ear-mounted speakers. Joe could also see the man was working very diligently to remove the Lincoln's stereo. The cranked up rap must have prevented the kid from hearing the obligatory warning, "FIVE-OH!"

This is gonna be fun, Joe thought. He let the light from his four-cell Mag Lite wash over the kid's hands as he pulled on wires and yanked on plastic.

"Yeah, that's it, shine it down here." The boy said, still half dangling out of the window. Joe had to bite his lip to keep from laughing. Then he moved the beam of light from the boy's hands to his face.

"Hey, man! What the fuck?" The light was blinding the kid. He couldn't see who was holding the light. Despite his protests, Joe kept the light right in his face.

When the boy finally removed his headphones and partially shielded his eyes from the intent glare, he saw Joe's badge.

"Hello, Albert..." Joe said.

Dumbstruck, the boy said, "Albert? Who's that?"

"You. Aren't you Albert Einstein?" Joe had a good laugh at that one. But, before he could thoroughly enjoy it, "Albert" started to fish his way out of the window. Joe grabbed his legs through the door.

"Hey, man! Get the fuck off of me!" The boy twisted and struggled and Joe held on with all the strength his five foot, five inches, one hundred and forty pounds could muster. Then the kid managed to claw his way to the passenger side door and pull himself forward. He pulled Joe too. Right through the window.

Joe reached for his portable radio, but when he loosened his grip, the boy got one leg free. And started kicking Joe in the face. Hard. Joe, now fully inside the car with the boy, began an awkward dance composed of weird wrestling moves and short, choppy punches. During one of their quick embraces, Joe heard the distinctive snap of the leather strap that held his Smith & Wesson .40 semi-automatic pistol in place. More fumbling. Before Joe knew what had happened, the kid had his gun and had it pointed right at him.

The boy eased his way out of the Lincoln and kept the gun trained on Joe. Joe instinctively put his hands in the air and began his negotiations.

"I said, shut the fuck up!" The boy screamed. The noise echoed. Mixed in with his cry, the boy could also hear the sound of another car, coming up on them fast. He turned to see it was another police car.

Seeing an opportunity while the kid's attention was diverted, Joe leapt for his gun. It went off. This noise too, echoed. Time stopped. The boy looked down, then looked over his shoulder to see the other police car screeching to a stop. He gripped the gun and ran like hell.

Lee Kole hopped out of his car, not sure what had happened. Had he heard a gunshot? He saw the boy running and took off after him, un-strapping his own pistol as he ran. When he passed the Lincoln, he noticed a body. Then he noticed it was his friend.

"JOE!" Kole stopped in his tracks, almost falling over himself with the momentum. Then he saw the blood. "Oh, shit! Joe! Speak to me!" Kole kneeled over his comrade and looked up for the running man. He saw nothing. He keyed his shoulder mic-he couldn't get through, someone was running a license plate. He keyed it again when he no longer heard the string of numbers and addresses. "BREAK!" He said to clear the traffic then, "102 to headquarters—10-100! I repeat—10-100! OFFICER DOWN!"

PROLOGUE—PART TWO

♦

January 14, 0005 Hours

Ashley Granger was tired. She should be. She had just worked a double shift at her job as an RN at Petersburg General Hospital. It was now a little after midnight and all she could think about was a hot shower, a hot meal and a warm bed. In that order.

She parked her silver Honda, hitched up her white skirt, and scratched her itchy support hose as she walked up the little brick walkway of her East Walnut Hill home on Fort Rice Street. It was a modest, two-bedroom, ranch style house; but since there was just her and Isis, her cat, it was more than enough.

Ashley fingered her house key from the big hoop ring in her purse. With her keys in one hand and her purse in the other, she looked up at her front door and noticed just how dark it was. She was sure she had left the porch light on before leaving this morning.

She lifted up her keys and motioned her hand toward the front door lock and began to press the key into the slot. But, when her key made contact with the lock, the door itself opened with a spooky, creaking noise. Then she noticed the little pieces of wood and shards of glass around the steps.

Nervously, Ashley used her left foot to open the door and with her right hand felt for the light switch on the wall, just inside. She flipped it. Nothing. But she could see a light inside-was it the kitchen?

She knew she shouldn't go in. She knew she should just go next door to Mrs. O'Reily's house and call the police. But this was her home, damn it, and no thieving kids were going to make her scared to go into her own damned house. She entered. Slowly.

As soon as she was standing in the living room, making her way toward the kitchen, she heard a rustling. Well, more of a scuffing along the carpet. It sure was dark. Then, suddenly a light flashed on from her right. The hallway light. She was stunned.

Standing there, partially silhouetted by the hall light and partially lit by the kitchen, was a man, completely nude-except for a pair of bright yellow gloves (were they her dishwashing gloves?) and a shower cap. As much as the sight of him startled Ashley, the sight of the large butcher's knife in his hand frightened her even more.

The man made some kind of gurgling, grunting noise and started to move toward her. He looked at her with a crazed, almost hungry look in his eye. She couldn't move.

The naked man with a knife was about ten feet away from her when he started to walk faster. The last thing that Ashley saw before she felt his hands on her throat was the gleam of light reflecting off of the very long blade.

CHAPTER 1

♦

January 14, 0058 Hours

Senior Police Officer Adam Styles stood brooding over the small conference table inside the Whale. The table had several maps scattered across it, detailing everything from property grids to city plumbing blueprints. The converted Petersburg Area Transit bus had been the home of the Petersburg Bureau of Police's Crisis Response Team Negotiators for as long as anyone could remember. He had been talking to the resident of 5901 Richmond Avenue, on the city's south end, for a little over an hour and forty minutes. Styles had just put on his uniform for his midnight shift when his C.R.T. pager went off.

The resident, Mr. Arnold "AC" Cowlings, had gotten drunk, had a fight with five family members and friends after dinner, then got an old .22 hunting rifle out of his bedroom closet and took everybody hostage in the living room. One of the family members, Aunt May, had been in the bathroom when all of the commotion started and called 911 from her cell phone. C.R.T. was immediately dispatched with Negotiators arriving on scene an hour before Tactical arrived.

Two heavily armed and heavily armored C.R.T. Tactical Team officers had taken a "throw phone" to the living room window when initial attempts of communication through telephone and bullhorn failed. The device was nothing more than a basic phone packaged in a thick, plastic box, with a 200 foot phone wire coming out of it and running back to an exact duplicate inside the Whale. It was durable and meant to actually be thrown through windows and other openings.

Looking down at the maps, Styles still cradled his end of the throw phone in his neck. Mr. Cowlings, it seemed, wanted one million dollars (in small bills of course) and a helicopter to land right in the middle of Richmond Avenue to make his escape. Upon hearing that getting the money might take some time, Mr. Cowling settled for a carton of cigarettes in exchange for the release of two people-his sister and his mother. They had been de-briefed by Sergeant Phil Johnson and Lieutenant Marlon Rollins, the C.R.T. Negotiator's co-leaders. According to mom and sis, AC had gotten drunk and started to become abusive. When one of his cousins (neither mom nor sis could remember which one) called him a "punk-assed bitch", AC went for the rifle.

"Look here, AC," Styles continued, "I've just gotten off the phone with my boss, and he says they've been able to round up about twenty thousand dollars from the First Community Pride Bank on Market Street, but that's all we've been able to come up with so far." This was a common negotiations technique: never say you can't get something done, blame it on someone else-your boss, the mayor, anyone-just buy time.

"Twenty thousand?" AC stammered through the phone. The trick seemed to have the desired effect. "Okay, well, if that's all you got."

"Now listen, AC," Styles pressed on with his ruse, "State police say that we can't get a helicopter to land here on Richmond Avenue, too many power and phone lines, but we can get one to land over in the Price-Mart parking lot." Styles waited for a response.

Nothing.

"AC, you still with me?"

"Yeah, I'm here…how am I gonna get to the Price-Mart?"

"Well, that's what I need to know, AC, I mean, we can take you there in an unmarked car, or we can call a cab, or—"

"Shit, man! You gonna get me in a police car? You'll take me to jail then!"

"No, no, AC, here's what we can do…" Styles was handed a slip of paper by Sergeant Johnson. It read,

Look at the window at the end of the house!!!

Styles looked out of the Whale. What he saw almost made him laugh out loud. Jumping to the ground out of the rear bedroom window and into the waiting arms of the TAC team were the hostages. One of the team members, Officer Gary Michaels, waved to Styles as he peered out. Michaels was one of Styles' closest friends in and out of the Bureau of Police. Styles saluted back in response.

"AC," Styles paused. "I just got a note-it says we can fly the helicopter over the house and roll out a rope ladder for you…" Styles waited, looking over to

Johnson who was on his radio to someone else. Johnson leaned over and hit the mute button on Styles's phone.

"TAC team confirms all hostages are out, Adam-it seems AC left everyone in the bedroom, then went into the kitchen to get another beer. He's been in the kitchen talking to you ever since. We're all clear."

"Jesus, Phil-what do you want to do now? Hang up and let the TAC team go get him?"

"Naw, just keep talking to him, let me talk to Captain Williams."

"Williams? Where's Lieutenant Rollins?"

Johnson paused just a little too long, then said, "Ahhh, he had to go-something's come up."

"Something's come up?!?" Styles was incredulous. "What could have *possibly* come up to make the Negotiations commander leave during an active negotiation?"

"I don't know, Adam-just keep him talking."

Styles turned back to the phone. Johnson released the mute. "AC, good news!" Styles said, "It looks like we've got you fifty thousand!"

"That's great man!" AC almost screamed. "Let's go! I'm ready! When do I get my money?"

As the TAC team moved into position around the Cowling's home, Sergeant Phillip Johnson came back to the Whale. He entered the rear section where Styles was still on the phone with AC. Johnson made a cutting motion across his neck to signal Styles to hit the mute button again.

"TAC is ready, time to change your approach," Johnson said.

"What do you mean?" Styles asked.

"Let him know he doesn't have anymore hostages and tell him if he doesn't come out, TAC would love to use him for target practice."

"But Phil, what if he decides to take himself out?" This was a valid concern. "Or even suicide by cop?"

Johnson fell silent for a long time. Then, "Adam, Joe Buckley was shot tonight. A little while ago. Most of the brass are leaving for Petersburg General right now."

"What?!?"

"We didn't want to tell you, as it might have affected your negotiations. As long as there were hostages, we didn't want you distracted."

"And now?"

"And now…fuck him. Wrap this up; TAC can handle this from here. I'm on my way to the hospital. As soon as you finish, come on up." Johnson headed for the exit.

"Phil!" Styles shouted, "How is he? How is Joe?"

"Don't know anything yet, Adam-only that he's been shot with his own gun and that he's alive. For now."

"I'm supposed to be working tonight, Phil. I'll finish this and head up to the E.R."

Johnson nodded and left. Styles turned back to his phone. Picking it up, he said, "AC, change of plans."

"Oh, yeah? You got me some more money?"

"No, you dumbass, go look in your bedroom."

"What you mean?"

"AC, I usually wouldn't be so blunt, but I just got word a friend of mine has been shot, so I've got to hurry up and end this thing. I'm looking at your criminal history right now, and I see you don't really have anything really bad on it," Styles scanned the printed page in front of him. "A few marijuana charges, couple of shopliftings, not much-so I'm gonna level with you."

AC was starting to sense something was wrong. His feeling was confirmed when he opened the door to his rear bedroom and found that everyone was gone. "Oh, shit, man!" He cried out over the phone.

"That's right, AC-deep shit." Styles answered. "Now, again, since you don't have much on your record, I want you to listen to me very carefully. You haven't hurt anyone tonight. No one in your family wants to press charges," Styles was winging it, figuring that at least half of A.C.'s family would want to press charges, "and no cops have been hurt either, so as of right now, you have a choice."

"What that is?"

"You can choose to come out right now, and we can end this with no one getting hurt, or you can choose to stay in there and all those guys with the black ninja suits and big guns come in there and make sure they hurt you." Styles paused for dramatic effect, "You have one minute to decide."

It wasn't much of a decision. After a lot of bitching and moaning, AC agreed to come out. The TAC team took him to the ground and cuffed him. A marked patrol unit took him away without incident. As Styles was shutting down the Whale, Captain Ronald Williams entered.

"Styles?" Williams called out.

"Back here, Captain." Styles acknowledged as he stowed away various communications gear.

"You've heard about what happened to Joe?"

"Yes sir, but only the basics. Care to fill me in?"

"Well, you probably know what I do-some kid got his gun away from him, shot him, and ran. He's in surgery now, and we're all going up to check on him." Williams looked around the inside of the Whale then his eyes fell back on Styles. "Adam, I know you're supposed to be on-duty tonight, and I know you're pretty drained dealing with Mr. Rocket Scientist in there, but I just want you to know that we're really going to need you on the streets tonight. Are you up to it?"

"Sure, Captain, what choice do I have?" Styles smiled, but there was in fact no other choice and Williams knew it. Manpower was always an issue with the Bureau, and tonight, with half the force here and with an officer down, the City needed all the police it could get.

Williams extended his hand, Styles shook it. "Get this tub put away and hit the streets." Williams offered a tight grin.

"Captain?" Styles asked as Williams was about to leave. "Is it alright if I stop by and see about Joe?"

"Adam, it's going to be pretty crazy tonight, but I'm not telling you 'no'; just make it quick once you call in."

"Yes sir." With that, Williams left and Styles hurried to finish packing away the equipment.

CHAPTER 2

◆

January 14, 0203 Hours

Lee Kole stood against the door frame to the Officer's Lounge just outside of the emergency room of Petersburg General Hospital. He looked down at his hands. His fingers and the French Blue cuffs of his uniform were caked with brownish-red dried blood. Joe Buckley's blood.

Across the hall from him were Lieutenant Marlon Rollins and Sergeant Phil Johnson-fellow officers and teammates of both Kole and Joe on the C.R.T. No one said a word. They had been waiting to hear something from the doctors ever since Joe was rushed into surgery.

Chief of Police Stanley Wayne Kyle and assorted captains and lieutenants were actually inside the Officer's Lounge with Joe's wife, Marcy. Kole had been relegated to his current outside position by both rank and importance. He looked over at his friends Phil and Marlon. No one said a word. He felt a hand on his shoulder and turned around. It was Adam Styles.

"Hey, big guy..." Styles tried to sound upbeat. Lee Kole along with Gary Michaels were Styles' best friends in the Bureau. Both of them gentle giants who, at over six feet each, towered over Styles' five-seven frame. "How's Joe?"

Kole was despondent, "Don't know, they won't tell me shit, Adam. All the brass is over there with Marcy-but no one will let me know a goddamned thing."

"How you holding up?"

"I guess I'm okay," Kole tried to sound convincing. "I just fucked up."

Looking up at his friend, Styles replied, "Lee, how did *you* fuck up? You didn't do anything wrong here."

"Adam!" Kole's face turned red, "Joe's fucking shot-I was his back up! I should have been there instead of fucking around at headquarters, I should have—"

"Stop right there, Lee," Styles put his hand on Kole's chest. "I'm not going to let you do this to yourself. This is not your fault, and you're not going to beat yourself up over it! Now you listen to me, this isn't your fault anymore than it's mine for being out in the Whale when all this went down! We're cops-we put our asses on the line every minute of every day we're out there. Joe knew that-and Joe knows whatever happened, it is not your fault! Some drone out there's got Joe's gun and we've got to get it back before someone else gets hurt." Styles saw that Kole was looking away. "Are you listening to me, man?"

Before Kole could answer, their radios sounded in unison, "102, 112." The dispatcher's voice echoed inside the emergency room. It was police headquarters calling Styles over his handheld police radio.

"102-112 and I are at the E.R.!" Style's voice barked back, relaying to whomever was behind the microphone at HQ they'd better goddamned not have some dumbass call for him, as he was currently awaiting news-any news-about Joe.

"102, 112…need you to be 10-8." The dispatcher said tensely, knowing exactly where Styles was and what he was doing. Life does go on, and right now there were no other officers available for this call. And really, what could Styles do by just sitting in the E.R.?

"That's a negative, headquarters," Styles spat out, "10-5." He requested a private chat on the police radio's channel two. He then excused himself from Kole, "Hang on a minute, Lee, let me tell these fucks we're busy!" Styles walked down the hall and around the nurses' station desk.

Police headquarters responded to Styles across the radio, "On two."

"Headquarters," he started out slow. Calm. "Be advised, I am 10-6 with Unit 112 in reference to unit 103. You remember 103, don't you? He's the cop who's been shot!" That last remark was mean and uncalled for, but it made Styles feel better by lashing out at somebody.

"102, be advised," the dispatcher's tone now sharp and biting, "all other units are tied up…per 100 Bravo, *you are 10-8!*" Well, that was it. 100 Bravo, Sergeant Scott Fisk, the midnight shift's duty supervisor had given the dispatcher the juice to yank them out of the hospital. *Where was Fisk anyway?* Styles thought to himself, noticing his absence at the hospital. *A cop on his shift gets shot and he's not here?*

"102, do you copy?"

Silence.

"Headquarters direct to unit One Zero Two. Do you copy that you are 10-8?"

Styles looked toward the ambulance entrance of the E.R. He saw a commotion. Orders were being shouted by doctors and medical staff. A police officer from the evening shift was running behind three EMTs and a stretcher. Behind them, yet another EMT was carrying bags and equipment. A young woman was on the stretcher. Styles recognized her as Ashley Granger, one of the Sexual Assault Nurse Examiners, or S.A.N.E. nurses assigned to the hospital. These were registered nurses who had specialized training in rape and sexual assault evidence collection. She had blood on what was left of her white uniform. A lot of blood. Styles keyed his mic.

"102, I copy. We'll be 10-8...Stand by..." He walked over to where the EMT's had parked Ashley's stretcher. There was a whirlwind of activity as medical people from what seemed like every department buzzed in and around her. Styles tapped the shoulder of the officer who had brought her in.

"What the hell happened?" Styles asked.

Officer John Tomas rubbed the bridge of his nose, "Shit, Adam, some sick fuck broke into her house, front door's all busted in." Thomas nodded to Ashley's stretcher, "He really did a number on her. She's lucky to be alive."

"Rape?" Styles said, more of a statement than a question.

"Yeah, looks that way." Thomas took a deep breath. "Her uniform was cut off her, right down the middle. Pieces of her bra and panties were found in her house, where the attack took place. Suspect slashed her throat and stabbed her...I don't...I don't know how many times."

"What do you mean 'in her house, where the attack took place'? Where did you find her?"

"After the attack, we think she tried to call the police—found blood all over her phone-but the lines were cut from the outside. She managed to crawl out the front door and over to a neighbor's house. That's when we got the call."

"Holy shit..." Styles whispered.

"How's Joe?" Thomas asked, switching gears.

"Don't know, they won't tell us a goddamn thing. Kole's been here since it went down and no one's told him anything." Just then, Styles's radio crackled again, "102, need this unit to be 10-8, 10-18."

Styles rolled his eyes at Thomas. "And now, I've got to put up with this shit!" Styles keyed his shoulder mic. "Go ahead with your call, headquarters."

"102, 112 respond to 42 Walta Circle…four, two Walta Circle for report of 10-60…complainant advised that he was at the movies and when he returned, he came home to find his place 10-60ed. Caller stated he has not yet entered his house-afraid someone may still be inside."

Great, Styles thought. *I gotta leave Joe and Ash to go take a stupid burglary?*

"Headquarters, are you advising this is a 10-60 *in-progress*?"

There was no response.

"Headquarters?"

Finally, "Negative, 102, caller advises that he is just scared to go back inside his house until officers arrive."

"10-4, headquarters, you can disregard 112, I'll take the call." Styles grumbled and turned. He saw Kole down the hallway, apparently listening to the radio traffic. Styles gave Kole a sign, letting him know that he'd handle whatever was going on over at Walta Circle. Kole nodded appreciatively. Styles looked over to Thomas.

"John, you let us know if you hear anything, right?"

Thomas patted him on the shoulder and gave Styles a thumbs-up. The giant automatic doors to the E.R. made a loud swooshing sound as Styles left.

CHAPTER 3

◆

January 14, 0224 Hours

Walta Circle was in the Berkley Manor subdivision on the city's south side. Since the burglary had already occurred and since he had to leave his friends in the hospital to respond to it, Styles was in no hurry to get there. He cruised up Sycamore Street at a slow pace. His mind kept drifting to the things that had happened recently to him during the past year. Since the summer, he had been involved in two high profile hostage negotiations. The first had so impressed the Crisis Response Team's Negotiations leader that he had asked him to join the team. He had also been promoted to Senior Police Officer, or SPO, and last, but certainly not least, began an illicit extra-marital affair with an old high school girlfriend. The fact that the girlfriend was now a dispatcher for the police department-and the daughter of the chief of police-only served to complicate matters.

Styles had always considered himself the straightest of arrows. He was an Eagle Scout, devoted husband, family man according to his all his friends and neighbors. Now it seemed, and although true, he did not want to admit it, he was an adulterer. He was a liar. He was a cheat. He had allowed his feelings for a pretty woman to interfere in basically every aspect of his life-work, home, leisure. But, as his best friends Officers Gary Michaels and Lee Kole told him, "way to go!" Mackenzie Kyle was a knockout. Not that his wife, Susan, was anything to sneeze at. Susan was what every man wanted in a wife-she had beauty, warmth, dependability…but with Mackenzie, there was heat. She was what every man wanted-period. Drop dead gorgeous looks, killer body, intelligence, humor. And for the life of him, Styles couldn't figure out just what the hell she saw in him.

Styles wasn't bad looking nor was he unlikable. Simply put, Styles just knew that he was not tall, dark, and handsome. Someone that Mackenzie should be attracted to. He was not the shortest officer in the department, but it was close. He was told by others that his dynamic personality and boyish good looks were why he got along with most anybody. That, and the fact that he could talk his way out of most any situation. Styles had that certain something that you just couldn't name. People liked him. Even people who didn't like him, liked him. It was this quality that made Lieutenant Rollins recruit him for the C.R.T. Negotiations team.

Styles was a smooth talker, fast-thinking on his feet, and quick-witted. His comments could charm a snake and his sarcasm could drip with venom. He was also quite competent with his weapon. Though a far cry from being the best shot in the Bureau, Styles qualified in the mid-nineties with his department-issued Smith & Wesson .40 caliber twice a year. But being a small guy on the mean streets of the midnight shift in a city twenty miles south of Richmond; along the I-95 drug corridor, Styles learned quickly to rely on his personal talents.

Many a night Styles had found himself on some street corner or dark alley surrounded by some of Petersburg biggest and toughest only ending up convincing them it was in their best interest to either surrender or walk away. Most times they did with a smile.

There was a tiny buzz from Styles' duty belt. He looked down at the vibrating alpha-numeric pager. There on the tiny illuminated screen was a message from Kyle:

Glad everything went well on Richmond…going to bed now, thinking of you. Miss you. Love you. OXOXOX

He couldn't help but be touched. Mackenzie was off tonight, and she must have been listening to her own radio or scanner. He'd call her first thing in the morning.

Styles finally found himself pulling up in front of 42 Walta Circle. A small crowd had gathered on the lawn. In the center, he noticed, were a man and woman-both in their underwear and bathrobes. *Neighborhood watch?* Styles laughed to himself as he grabbed his in-dash radio. "102 to headquarters, mark me 10-6 on Walta Circle."

As he got out of his cruiser, Styles now noticed that the man and woman were arguing. Stepping right into the middle of the fray, he wondered if it was such a good idea to leave Lee Kole behind. His mere presence would serve this crowd well.

"Excuse me folks." Styles pulled out his black, four-cell flashlight and flooded the yard with light. The crowd started to disperse with the appearance of the black and white patrol car. He addressed them in a loud voice, "Who called the police?"

"I did, Officer!" The man in the underwear and bathrobe said.

"He did not, Officer, I did!" The woman in the bathrobe countered.

Styles held up his hands. "One at a time, please. Sir, what's going on here?"

"I'll tell you what's going on, Officer. I live here, see? This is my house!" The man walked briskly up to his porch and pointed to his front door. "See this? See this?" He was shouting now. "Ask *her* how this happened!"

Styles turned to the woman, whose slipping bathrobe was beginning to show more than it was supposed to out in the open air. "Ma'am? Do you live here? And please, secure your, ah…robe?"

She adjusted herself and said, "Yes, sir-I do! I rent a room from this man here and my boyfriend came by to see me!"

"At one o'clock in the morning?" The man interrupted. His robe simply hung open, revealing his dirty boxer shorts.

"Sir, please let her finish," Styles chastised him.

"Yes, let me finish! Thank you!" The woman continued. "Anyway, my boyfriend came over and when I opened the door, this fool won't let him in-see, he's jealous of my new boyfriend 'cause we used to talk too."

"You and this man here used to date?" Styles tried to clarify.

"Yeah, we used to date, and have *relations*, if you know what I mean-but he gets so damned jealous! Where you be? Where you been? I tell him, I be where I'm at!"

"So why are you still living here?" Styles asked.

"'Cause she ain't got nowhere else to go! That's why!"

"Oh, shut up, you old fool!"

"Where's your new boyfriend now, Ma'am?" Styles asked.

"Well, once he broke down my damned door, he left!" The man yelled.

"He didn't break down your damned door—I did!" The woman yelled back.

"Why'd you do that, Ma'am?"

"When this fool wouldn't let Marquis in, I went outside to talk to him on the porch. Then, he slams the door and locks me out! Well, I didn't have my key! So I started banging on the door-but he wouldn't let me in!" She closed the robe tightly around her. "So, I tells Marquis to break it down-but he won't do it-so I start kicking and slamming on it, finally, it opens! Well, this fool's done called the police on me. Marquis split and here we are!"

A few of the crowd's stragglers started to snicker and whisper among themselves. Styles decided he'd had enough. Turning to the man he said, "Sir, does she live here?"

"Not anymore, I'm throwing her out!"

"Sir, does she have anything in this house that belongs to her? Clothes? Shoes? Stuff like that?"

"Well, yeah…"

"Well, sir-you just can't throw her out. She also can't be charged with breaking into her own property. This is what we call a civil matter."

"What that is?" The man asked, obviously upset.

"That means I can't make her leave anymore than I can make you leave. You'll have to go down to the courthouse tomorrow morning and file papers to start the eviction process if you want her out."

"But it's my house!" The man protested.

"I understand that, sir, but she lives here. This is not a criminal matter."

"HA! HA! You old fool!" The woman began to laugh.

"Ma'am, if I were you, I'd still get some of my things and go somewhere else tonight. I'll tell you both right now, if I have to come back, I'm going to arrest both of you for disturbing the peace. Do I make myself clear?"

They both nodded as louder murmurs rippled through the crowd. "And the rest of you go back to your homes!" Styles looked around, "Unless you want me to start running warrant checks on all of you." That sent everyone back where they came from. Styles turned to the couple, "It's almost three in the morning. Let's call it a night. Go to bed. Fix this in the morning, okay?"

The two didn't say anything, but did silently head back into the house. Styles could hear the sound of the man trying to secure his front door with the inside chain.

CHAPTER 4

♦

January 15, 1420 Hours

Kermit Epstein was a scrawny, little white boy. At fifteen, he was only five foot, four inches and didn't weigh one hundred pounds soaking wet. He was, however, a very bright child. Brilliant, in fact, according to his teachers at Peabody Middle School. Kermit was one of only twenty-four white kids in his ninth grade class. He was the only Jewish one.

Kermit, or "K-Dawg", as he was called by what he liked to think of as his friends, belonged to a loose group of kids who didn't beat him up (much) and allowed him to hang out with them-as long he let them cheat off him during tests and as long as he helped out (that usually meant doing their homework). It wasn't easy being a gansta'.

Kermit was standing outside Byrd's Convenience Store shivering. Even though his obligatory black Oakland Raiders jacket was completely buttoned up and its hood raised over his head, the temperature was only twenty-two degrees in the middle of the afternoon.

Kermit was waiting for his friend Drequel "Dre" Sanders. Dre was three years older than Kermit, but was a lot more immature. Dre had text messaged Kermit thirty minutes ago on his cell phone. Dre had told him to meet him here at the corner of Harding Street and Saint Matthew Street, that he had something important to tell him.

Well, he'd better get here fast; I'm freezing my ass off! Kermit thought to himself. Out of the corner of his eye, he saw a blur of black. Dre was crouching down behind two garbage cans between a row of houses on Virginia Avenue. Dre, too, had on his Raider's jacket. Dre stayed hunkered down behind the cans. He whistled and waved to Kermit.

Kermit looked around as if they both were being watched. By the way Dre was acting, Kermit thought perhaps they were.

"Get over here, fool!" Dre yelled as softly as he could-in an almost screaming whisper.

Kermit crossed the street and joined Dre in-between the houses. He leaned up against the rusting aluminum siding. "What up, dog?" Kermit asked his buddy.

"Listen up, K-Dawg," Dre began, his voice still low, his eyes darting left to right. "I need you to do something for me."

"What up?"

Dre reached into his jacket and pulled out a red dishtowel. Kermit looked down, he could see that the within the towel was something wrapped tightly. Dre opened the towel. Kermit leaned in then stepped back until he hit the siding again.

"Where did you get that?" Kermit asked in a whisper to match Dre's.

"I uh…" Dre struggled for the words, "I found it-over by the fairgrounds." He pushed it toward Kermit. Kermit would not take it.

"I need you to hold onto it for a while," Dre asked more than stated.

"Nuh, uh, man. No way!" Kermit put his hands in his jacket's pockets.

"Listen, nigga," Dre's voice was more firm now, commanding. "I *need* you to hang on to this piece for me-just a little while!" Dre forced it forward again. Kermit slowly put out his hands.

"Here." Dre shoved the gun into Kermit's grip. "Take this home. Hide it. I'll get it back from you later. Understand?" Dre's eyes locked on Kermit's. Kermit noticed the intensity in Dre's stare. He also noticed the bead of sweat forming over Dre's brow, despite the low temperature.

Kermit held the gun. He turned it around in his hands. Then he saw it. It has been scratched over-maybe with a screwdriver or a butter knife-but it was still there. He looked up a Dre. "Man, why don't you just toss this into a lake? Or down the sewer?"

"You stupid, man?" Dre looked shocked. "That's a nice gun-not like that shit that Boo carries or the crap we usually see the Uptown Boys got."

Kermit had to agree. With the exception of the new scratches it was immaculate. "Okay, Dre-you right. Those Uptown boys ain't got nothing like dis!" Kermit said, referring to the rag-tag street gang that usually inhabited the area they were in currently.

"I'm say'n!" Dre confirmed. "So, you cool?"

Kermit re-wrapped the towel loosely around the shiny metal, then stuck it into his own jacket.

"Alright, Dawg-I gotta jet. I'll holler later!" Dre held out his fist. Kermit made his own fist and lightly tapped Dre's in their urban handshake. With that, Dre slinked off down the alley and disappeared into the blighted neighborhood.

Kermit waited a few minutes, looked around again and then pulled the gun back out. He unwrapped it and turned it over to look at it again. On the slide portion of the pistol, engraved and very visible through the half-assed scratches, were the words:

PETERSBURG BUREAU OF POLICE

CHAPTER 5

♦

January 15, 1834 Hours

Adam Styles turned over and held the beautiful young redhead in his arms. They lay together, spent. Through the window of their room at Richmond's elegant Regal Hotel, Styles could see the city's nighttime skyline come to life.

"Whatcha doin'?" Mackenzie asked, her voice muffled against his shoulder and her pillow. Styles leaned in and kissed her cheek.

"Nothing…just thinking." Styles was thinking a lot lately. A lot about his life and where it was going. He had been married to Susan for so long-and he truly did love her-but was he happy? Was he in love with his wife? They fought so much, and over the smallest, stupid things.

She snuggled in closer, letting out a small sigh. "Wanna know what I'm thinking?" Her hand began to make small circles across his bare chest, centering on his right nipple. He took her hand and held it against the beating of his heart.

"I know exactly what you're thinking," Styles said with a smile. "And you'll have to give me about twenty more minutes…" He stroked her hair. "Listen, Mackenzie," his voice trailed off. She sat up lazily and turned to look at him. She arched her eyebrows.

"What are we doing here?" He asked solemnly.

"Well, I thought I was here making love to the most wonderful man in the world," she purred with her best mischievous grin. Styles couldn't help but get caught up in her gaze.

"You know what I mean, Mac-this is…this is wrong."

Mackenzie's face quickly lost its fanciful quality, replaced with a shade of pure anger. "Goddamn it, Adam-what do you want from me? Huh? Really, I have never asked you to leave your wife-even though you know that is what I want! I let you fuck me whenever you want-only because I am totally in love with you and I'll take you anyway I can have you! I mean-shit!" She covered herself up with a sheet and put a few feet between them in the bed. "We never get to go out and do anything that couples do-we never go to the movies or even walk through the park! It's always hotel rooms and my place-and the only time you start to show regret is after we've fucked! Well, I'm sorry, Adam-I love you! I'll do whatever you want, but you've got to stop this nonsense! Please!" She actually huffed as she exhaled heavily.

"Mackenzie, I'm...I'm sorry, I didn't-"

"No, Adam, you never do!" She retorted. "Look, if you want me to go away, just tell me! I'm a big girl! I'll go away!"

Styles cringed at those words. Although he knew what they were doing really was wrong, and he knew it was bound only for disaster, the last thing he wanted was for Mackenzie Kyle to go away. She made him feel loved. She made him feel wanted. Deep in his heart, not to mention more obvious body parts, she made him feel alive.

"Mackenzie..." Styles paused, thinking very hard about the next words he was about to say. "I love you."

Mackenzie Kyle stared at him with her eyes widening. She did not say a word. Styles moved in closer, cupped his hands under her chin and held her face in his hands. "Did you hear me? I said I love you." He kissed her on her nose. "I know things are all fucked up right now, and I know that I've been pretty fucked up too...but the bottom line is, you are the best thing that has ever happened to me and you are the best thing in my life. I don't know where we're going and I don't know how we're going to get there, but just know this one simple fact: I love you."

"Wow."

"Wow?" Styles laughed. "That's it? I confess my undying love for you and all you can come up with is 'wow'?"

Mackenzie sat up even straighter, letting the sheet fall to her lap. Her arms shot straight out, grabbed Styles, and with all her strength, pulled him into her. She kissed him hard. She kissed him with a desperation and an urgency that she had never felt before. Styles kissed back just as passionately.

"Honey?" She whispered as her hands caressed his body.

"Yes, beautiful?" He felt her hands go down further.

"I don't think I'm going to have to wait twenty minutes."

CHAPTER 6

♦

January 15, 2255 Hours

Every time a patrol shift began its tour, the officers all assembled for roll call. This brief and usually informal gathering was the time for beat assignments and general updates. The shift commander and assistant squad leader would recite information on stolen cars to be on the lookout, or BOL, for, as well as pass along any additional information that the front line troops needed for their patrols. Usually, Roll Call was the time and place for a little smoking and joking.

Tonight, the Roll Call room of the Patrol Division was particularly quiet. In light of the events of the past few days, no one felt much like joking. Even the customary black humor that the cops were known for fell by the wayside in the wake of the shooting of their fellow officer and the brutal rape of a well-liked nurse.

Even Sergeant Fisk, who tried to open every Roll Call session with a joke-no matter how lame-simply entered the room and sat down at the head of the long conference table. The men and women of the 100-Bravo midnight shift all sat with their heads down and awaited the bulletins and announcements.

"Good evening everyone," Sergeant Fisk began as he exhaled. "First, I want to let everyone know about Joe." Everyone looked up from their notepads. "It's a good news, bad news situation, people." Fisk paused, apparently for dramatic effect, and then continued. "The good news is it looks like Joe's gonna be alright. At least, that is to say, he's gonna live. He's not out of the woods yet, folks-but he's stable and the docs all say things are looking good for him."

"Can we go see him yet, Sarge?" Officer Denton asked, her voice cracking a bit with the question. "Is he conscious? Alert?"

"Not yet, Susanne, he's in and out. The family has requested no visitors until he comes out of ICU…uh, no flowers, please."

"And Ashley?" Officer Mike Chavez inquired.

Fisk's face grew a shade grimmer. "The news is not so good for her. She lost a lot of blood and there was severe head trauma…she's in a coma…" his voice trailed off. "It's fifty-fifty."

Everyone remained silent.

"In other news," Assistant Squad Leader Cecil Perkins flipped through the clipboard in front of him, searching for items to share with the officers. "Be advised, we've had another sighting of the Southside Weenie Wagger." Perkins's description solicited a few laughs around the otherwise sober table.

"Where did he strike this time, Cecil?" Officer Gary Michaels, a big lug of an officer, had a sideways grin.

"Says here in the window of the All-For-A-Dollar Store in the 2600 block of South Crater Road." Perkins ran his finger down a photocopied report. "Apparently he stood on the sidewalk outside of the business and exposed himself to two teenage girls inside. As usual, he ran when they went to the front to tell the management."

"Any further description?" Styles choked back a laugh.

"No, nothing's changed-white male, late 30's to early 40's, dark hair, average build."

"Don't forget, huge crank." Michaels chimed in. This got even more laughs.

"Okay, okay, people…" Fisk interjected. "This guy has been exposing himself to women and young girls all over the south side. Every time it's between the hours of 1800 and 0200 hours. He's pulled it out in front of girls as young as ten, people-that's not funny. We need to get this pervert, and fast!" Fisk looked around the room. "Town units and 4-patrol, pay special attention to any single male walking alone in the south end of the city!"

Roll Call continued with the usual BOL's for stolen cars and wanted suspects. Styles mindlessly wrote down the information, but his thoughts were elsewhere. He could still smell Mackenzie's perfume on his hands, her scent lingering. What was he going to do? What were his real alternatives? Realistically, what could he do? Leave his wife? Move in with Mackenzie? None of those options seemed right.

"Styles!" Fisk's voice was harsh and shook Adam from the grip of his thoughts.

"Yessir?" Styles snapped back to attention.

"Keep an ear out downtown for anyone with info on Joe or Joe's gun. I know you have a...shall we say, 'a relationship' with a lot of those kids in the area from your S.T.A.R. days." Fisk was referring to the anti-drug and violence program in the city's public schools called Students Together Are Responsible. Styles had a brief stint as an S.T.A.R. Officer when the former policeman assigned to that position was caught having sex with one of his students. That officer ended up killing himself after a failed negotiation by Styles and the CRT negotiators.

"Yeah, Adam," Michaels added, "talk to some of your little angels and see if they'll help you out," he snorted. "I'm sure you taught them well."

"Hey, hey, hey!" Styles jokingly protested, "I just taught them not to shoot *me* when they grow up! They could care less about 'just say no'. But I'll see what I can do, Sarge."

"Alright, everyone-let's hit the streets." Fisk dismissed the group.

As the uniformed officers filed out of the Roll Call room, Styles felt his pager buzz again. It was, of course, her.

CHAPTER 7

♦

January 15, 2310 Hours

The thin wisps of smoke spiraled up from the burning paper as Dre passed the blunt to Kermit. Kermit did not particularly enjoy marijuana, either the smoking of it or the after effects, but it seemed that his peers could not get enough of it.

"Mmmmm…" Dre sighed, "That's some good shit, there."

"Uh, huh." Kermit replied as he took the cigarette and inhaled. He tried in vain to suppress a cough, but the harder he tried, the more it came out in loud, smoke-filled bursts.

Dre laughed out loud. "Damn, K-Dawg, you buggin'!" Kermit smiled through clenched teeth. He reached across the dirty floor they were sitting on-Dre's bedroom was a complete dump. His bare, stained mattress lay on an equally filthy floor. Fast food wrappers mixed with the discarded garbage of a teenaged thug. Trash and scraps littered the rest of the tiny room he shared with his mother and four siblings on High Pearl Street.

The two had been drinking and smoking for the past half hour and Kermit had something on his mind. He wanted to tell Dre that he knew about the gun and where it came from, but he was afraid. Hell, if Dre had shot that cop, would he even think twice about capping him? Kermit thought not. No, he'd wait until Dre had a little more booze in his stomach and a little more dope in his lungs. Kermit had found that Dre was a happy drunk. Quite mellow, in fact. When Dre got to drinking, he became more friendly and open to new ideas. Kermit passed the blunt back to him.

"Here man," Kermit said, "smoke up." He coughed again.

The two continued drinking and smoking, and then drinking some more until finally Kermit thought he had an opening. Dre was talking about a shooting a few months ago, where some of the Uptown Boys had shot a friend of theirs, Tyrone "Willy-Tee" Willis.

"Man, I ain't *never* seen so much blood as that day Willy-Tee got shot!" Dre was reminiscing. "Never!" The two laughed through the smoky haze.

"Dre..." Kermit started out slowly.

Dre simply arched his eyebrows in response, his lids heavy with drug-induced sleepiness.

"Dre..." Kermit tried again. "I've been looking at that gun you gave me."

Dre's eyes shot open-no friendly, happy drunk look in them now.

"What about it?" Dre asked very deliberately, with a trace of menace.

"Well, I've been looking at it." Kermit replied calmly, but his calm was fading fast. "And I saw where someone had filed off something on the barrel...you can still read it."

"What?" Dre sat up, rigid now fully alert. "Why you do that for?"

"Now, listen, Dre," Kermit held his hands up in mock surrender, "don't go getting all mad at me and shit!" Kermit backed away from Dre. "It's just that with that cop getting shot-it's been in all the papers and on T.V. and stuff. The gun says Petersburg Police on the side..." Kermit chose his next words very carefully. "Did *you* shoot that cop?"

Like a rocket, Dre was up and slammed Kermit against the wall so hard that two framed pictures of Dre's favorite rappers fell to the floor. "You shut the fuck up!" Dre hissed, his hands at Kermit's throat.

Kermit thought fast. He spoke even faster. "Look, Dre-its okay, its okay! I didn't tell no one-I didn't tell *nobody*!" Kermit tried to slip his fingers under Dre's tightening grip. "I just wanted you to know that I knew-and that I ain't gonna tell nobody!"

Dre stared at Kermit through bloodshot eyes. It seemed an eternity before he spoke again. "What if I did shoot that cop?" His voice was just above a whisper.

Kermit started to breathe again. "It's cool, Dre, it's cool...I was just thinkin'."

"You was thinkin' what?" Dre demanded.

"Well, you know Dre," Kermit stammered. "That gun's pretty hot. If they catch you or me with it, they'll put us away for life, man! We need to get rid of it-fast!"

"You threw my damn gun away?" Dre's hands were back at Kermit's throat.

"No, no, Dre—I'm just sayin' we should get rid of it, soon."

Dre relaxed his grip again. "Why we gots to get rid of the gun? I filed down the numbers and shit!"

"Dre!" Kermit said. "Whatever you used-it didn't do anything but scratch up the metal. Even I could read the goddamned 'PETERSBURG POLICE' on it! We need to get rid of it so that they won't know it was you who shot that cop. No gun, no evidence. See?"

Dre did not see. Dre could not see through his drug- and alcohol-induced state. The only thing that Dre saw was that shiny new gun. A gun that was better than anything anyone else was carrying around these parts. Through visions and dreams that only the drunk and stupid have, Dre saw that with that gun he was going places.

"Where's the gun now?" Dre asked.

"I gots it back at my house."

"Go get it."

"Now?" Kermit sounded both excited and scared.

"Yeah, now, fool! Go get me that gun, and I'll show you what we can do with it!"

Kermit did not like the sound of that. "What you gonna do, Dre?"

Dre looked at the clock on his dirty wall. "It's almost 11:30, the Quickie Mart should be pretty busy."

"So?"

"So, fool, we gonna hit it."

Kermit looked at his drunk friend. "Dre, that's not a good idea, man."

"Why the fuck not?"

"Well, for one thing, we're both too fucked up!" Kermit forced a smile and a laugh.

Dre did not laugh back.

Kermit continued to try to persuade Dre. "Look, man, you don't wanna rob no Quickie Mart anyway!"

"Why don't I?"

"Because, Dre, they ain't got no money! Maybe thirty or fifty dollars at anytime! All that money's in the safe!" Kermit thought for a moment. "Nah, if you wanna hit something-and I'm with you on that-we need a better target. And not tonight. Let's plan something for tomorrow or the next night. Let me see what else is out there."

This seemed to satisfy Dre. His eyelids were becoming heavy again.

"Okay, K-Dawg…you figure something out." Dre said, his speech a little slurred. Kermit was amazed at the speed with which Dre's mood could change. "Why don't you take off and I'll catch you in the A.M.?"

Kermit did not need to be told twice. "Alright, man," Kermit held up his fist to Dre's, "I'll check you later."

CHAPTER 8

◆

January 16, 0234 Hours

"Headquarters, can you 10-9 the description?" Styles spoke into the dash-mounted radio of his police package Ford Crown Victoria.

"10-4, 102; suspect is described as a bravo-mike, wearing all black clothing." The police dispatcher sounded as disinterested as Styles felt. "And what is the nature of the 10-15?" He asked, referring to the ten-code for a generic disturbance.

"That's unknown, 102, be advised, caller stated subject was on the corner of Sycamore and Washington Streets, flagging down cars...causing 10-15. No further."

Styles keyed his mic as he replaced it into its cradle, "10-4, show me 10-76 in the area." Styles was now canvassing the corners looking for this unknown black male causing an unknown disturbance.

"112 direct to 102, I'm about five minutes from you." Lee Kole's voice came over the radio.

Styles responded, "10-4, I got nothing showing..." Then he saw a possible suspect. "Headquarters, show me 10-6 in front of the SubStop on Sycamore."

"10-4, 102, 112, do you copy?"

"10-4, headquarters, I'm still en route."

Styles noticed the man was in fact wearing all black clothing and as his marked unit drove by, the man seemed to turn away. Styles hit his side alley lights, mounted in his overhead lightbar, spotlighting the man. He got out of his vehicle.

"Excuse me, sir?" Styles asked the man in his best polite/official voice. The man paid him no attention as he continued walking away from him, down Sycamore toward downtown.

"Sir!" Styles shouted, this time politeness fading. The man hesitated then took off in a sprint. Styles gave chase.

"102 to Headquarters!" Styles shouted into his shoulder mic, "I'm 10-80F, heading northbound on Sycamore, approaching Franklin Street!"

BEEEEEEEEEEEEEEEEEEEP! The alert tone sounded across Styles's radio and everyone else tuned into that frequency. The high pitched wail indicated that an emergency situation had developed; in this case, a foot pursuit, in which an officer was chasing a fleeing suspect. The dispatcher's voice was loud and deliberate, "All units, channel one is 10-3, channel one is 10-3. Unit 102 is 1080F northbound on Sycamore Street, approaching Franklin." The dispatcher was advising that no further radio traffic would be conducted unless having to do with the foot pursuit. "Unit 112?"

"112, I copy and am responding code three from Union Street." Lee Kole pressed his foot down hard on the accelerator as he simultaneously flipped on his overhead blue lights and siren.

Styles's voice came across the radio again, "102, we're in the alley behind the Daily Progress Building!" Styles was closing in on the runner when the man slipped on a spread of discarded newspapers. The unknown suspect then started to fall forward and roll over-still going with the momentum, until he hit a series of aluminum trash cans that lined the wall of the alley. With a loud crash the man was down; Styles was on top of him in an instant.

"Get on the ground!" Styles ordered to the man, as he rolled him over onto his face and struggled to get his handcuffs out. As he was fighting to clamp them on, he heard Lee Kole's police car come to a screeching halt and his siren stop. Kole bounded from the car and into the alleyway. "Adam, you alright? You got him?"

Clicking the cuffs locked and getting to his feet, Styles brushed off his midnight blue uniform. "Yeah, I'm fine," he looked down at the man, still on the ground, "fucker took off running right when I pulled up."

Kole held up his hand and grabbed his radio. "112 to headquarters, you can clear the channel-I'm 10-6 with 102, he's 10-95." Kole advised that all was okay and the suspect was in custody.

"Thanks," Styles said.

"So, uh…" Kole looked at the man on the ground, "what's the charge?"

"Huh?" Styles looked at his friend, his heart still pumping with adrenaline.

Kole laughed, "I know he ran-and you chased him, but now he's in hand-cuffs. What's the charge?"

Styles smiled and let out a forced laugh. "Well, right now, its contempt of cop! And besides, he's not *under arrest*. He is in investigatory detention! Now, help me get him up!"

The two cops picked the man up effortlessly-he seemed to weigh almost nothing.

"Alright, man," Styles began, "Why'd you run?" Kole began a pat down search of the suspect.

"Adam," Kole stated, "I've got something here." Kole was patting down the front of the suspect's pants. "Whach'a got in here, huh? Some dope? Some crack?"

The suspect spoke for the first time, "Naw, man! OWCH! Shit, man! Be careful!"

Kole looked over to Styles; they shared a confused look.

"What's wrong with you, I didn't hurt you!" Kole asked.

"Damn man! Just don't touch...uh, down there..."

Kole patted the man's crotch area again, "Down here?"

"SHIT! Man, that hurts!"

Styles walked closer to the man. "What's up here, man? What's going on down there?"

The man's eyes darted back and forth from Styles to Kole. "Okay, okay, man...I uh," he was sweating hard, beads of perspiration falling to the ground, "I got the drippy-dick, okay?"

Styles stared blankly at him. "The what?"

"Drippy-dick, drippy-dick! I gots the drippy-dick!" Seeing that the two cops didn't know what he was talking about, the man said, "Pull my pants down, you'll see!"

Styles looked cautiously at Kole, who was smirking. Styles reached around to the side of his black, leather duty belt and pulled a pair of latex gloves from a pouch. After putting them on, he reached down to the man's loose fitting trousers and unsnapped the button fly. The dirty pants fell to his knees.

Styles looked down, not quite sure what he was seeing. Kole jerked his neck around to see too. Looking down, the men saw that their suspect had a clear, plastic bag, similar to those used for sealing sandwiches or other foods, tied around his penis with a blue rubber band. The bag had traces of a yellowish fluid dripping around the folds.

"Oh, Christ, Adam, he's got gonorrhea!"

"Yeah!" The man exclaimed, "drippy-dick!"

Styles grimaced, "Damn, man-why don't you go to the health department-get a shot? Get that cleared up?"

Kole chimed in, "Yeah, buddy-they got medicine for that!"

"I know, I know-I just haven't got a chance to get by."

"Haven't had a chance?" Styles asked. "It's right down the street! You don't have time to go get a shot, but you can tie a bag around your dick?"

"Why'd you run, man?" Kole again asked.

"I gots papers on me," the man said, his head down.

"What kinds of papers?" Styles asked, reaching for his radio.

"Oh, just some damn baby's momma drama!"

"What does that mean?" Kole poked him. "Domestic assault?"

"Hell, no, man!" The suspect said, "I ain't ever hit no woman!"

"What's your name?" Styles continued.

"Steve Manfred."

"DOB?"

The man gave Styles his date of birth and Styles ran his information through headquarters. The dispatcher came back on the radio with a hit confirmation for Steve Manfred. He was wanted on a capias for failing to pay child support. Styles acknowledged the hit.

"Okay, Steve, you were right, I gotta serve this paper on you." Styles escorted Manfred back to his squad car. Kole got back into his.

"Hey, Steve…" Kole called out to the man. The man lifted his head. "You really need to go see the doctor!" Kole sped off from the scene.

"What did he mean by that?" Manfred asked Styles as he was being put into the back seat of the police vehicle.

"I guess he means that if you don't see a doc soon, your dick might fall off!"

"Really?"

"Really." Styles slammed the rear door and hopped back into the front seat for the drive down to the city jail.

After booking Mr. Drippy Dick, Styles cleared from the jail and headed one block up toward police headquarters.

"102," Styles spoke into his microphone.

"102," came the dispatcher's reply.

"10-8 from 40 Henry Street, suspect incarcerated. I'll be out at headquarters, dropping off paperwork."

"10-4, 102."

Styles parked his car in a slot directly behind HQ, and as he was about to get out of his vehicle, his radio sprang to life again.

"Delta 41, 10-5 with unit 102." It was the voice of Sergeant Billy Hancock. Hancock was the field leader of the Bureau's Street Crime Unit, or S.C.U.

Styles switched over to channel two on his portable radio and keyed his shoulder mic. "Go ahead, Delta 41."

"Are you clear?"

"I'm at Headquarters dropping off reports, but I'm clear. Whadda you got?"

"We're down at the Starlite Motel at Washington and Crater-we've got a few folks in need of a ride. We're all full, can you transport?"

"10-4, Delta 41, let me drop off this paperwork at the front desk, and I'll be en route."

"Do you have a cage?"

"10-4."

"Good. You might need it with these guys."

Styles took the stairs from the Tabb Street side entrance two at a time and bounded up to the front desk level. As he approached the main window, he noticed Mackenzie at the radio console behind the safety glass. She brushed her hair back out of her face and gave him a quick wave and a wink. This small gesture sent his heart racing.

Styles squinted, pursed his lips, and blew her a kiss. He was going for suave but he always came off as dorky. She laughed, as dorky was why she fell in love with him. She reached into the air, and made a little grabbing motion as if to catch the airborne kiss. He smiled and slid his reports through the open slot at the desk. A very stern looking Regina Hunt took the papers and gave him a scowl that matched Mackenzie's smile in intensity.

"Good evening to you too, Ms. Hunt." Styles tried to ply her with his charm.

"Mmm hmmm…" she said through tight lips. She was not one to be charmed.

Styles looked back to Mackenzie and mouthed "Gotta go now" as he thumbed toward the rear steps. She blew him a kiss back and nodded. He pretended to catch her kiss in mid air as well.

Back in his police car, Styles floored the accelerator, "102 to headquarters, I'm 10-8 from 10-19, and I'm 10-76 to the Starlite Motel."

Styles piloted his police cruiser through empty streets and deserted alleys until he hit the intersection of Washington Streets at Crater Road. Here, in this tiny section of the city, each street corner was littered with small hotels. No national chains, just cheap, locally owned flop houses that would rent by the hour if it wasn't against state law.

Styles couldn't even remember how many search warrants he'd done in these dirty little boxes that served only to house the local riff raff and drug dealers along with the working girls and whatever poor out of town sucker that happened off the interstate.

The Starlite Motel came into view, its antacid pink trim illuminated by the red and green of the traffic lights. Styles hit his rear deck lights and parked his car askew in front of the manager's office. A small crowd of locals had pooled around the parking lot looking up at the second floor of the two-storied stucco building. Styles saw a cluster of large men with flashlights overhead. Their camouflage pants and black jerseys gave the S.C.U. member away. That and the giant POLICE written in reflective white stitching on their backs.

Styles chuckled to himself at the design of the official duty uniform of the Street Crime Unit. Here in an urban cityscape, the woodland camouflage seemed out of place. But, Styles admitted to himself, when you have a man dressed in black and cammo, complete with a gunbelt and combat boots, the image was intimidating-as it was meant to be. *Criminals are a cowardly, superstitious lot…*Styles thought back to the reason Bruce Wayne decided to dress up like a giant bat to fight crime.

"Yo! Adam!" The bellowing voice of Howie Walters came down from above, "Up here!"

"I see you!" Styles held on to the not-so-secure metal railing as he ascended the white steps up to the second floor. When he reached the team, he began the usual cop shucking and jiving session with his fellow officers. After a few barbs and good natured insults, he poked his head into the room. The smell of burning hemp was overpowering.

Styles scanned the room. Five men were sitting on the floor, each one bound with plastic flexcuffs. The men were lined up against the far wall. In the middle of the room, various gym bags and duffles were being turned inside out and on the large, circular motel table, three piles of booty were growing.

One pile was for cash. Ten and twenty dollar bills were separated next to a pile of what appeared to be plastic bags filled with a greenish-brown leafy substance as well as other bags with small white rocks. Marijuana and crack cocaine. Not the score of a lifetime, but plenty to be sure. The third pile seemed to be a hodgepodge of rolling papers, razor blades, condoms, and empty plastic bags of various sizes.

Styles saw Hancock. "Hey, Billy," Styles called out. Even though Hancock was a sergeant and proper Bureau command etiquette would not be to address him by his first name, Styles knew that Billy hated being thought of as a supervisor. He'd much prefer to be in the field with the men, doing the dirty work. "Where do you need me?"

Hancock turned and said, "Hey, man…I need you to transport those last two on the end. Everyone else is coming with us back to Fourth Street." Fourth Street was the home of the Police Annex Building that housed the Vice/Narcotics, S.C.U., and Detective divisions along with the Evidence and Property offices. If Hancock was taking the other three with them it meant that they were going to be recruited for some involuntary undercover work to work off some charges. The fact that the other two were being taken directly to jail without passing Go or collecting $200.00 meant that they weren't playing ball.

Hancock spoke again, "I really appreciate this, Adam. Me, Sugarbear, and Sneak are heading over to the Goodnight Inn after this, and Howie and rest of the crew are going to be debriefing these humps. I've already been down to the magistrate's office and secured the warrants; I just need you to serve them and process these guys."

"No, problem, Billy." Styles looked at the two. He leaned a little closer, thinking that he recognized one of the suspects. He directed his gaze to the slender one on the end. "Hey, man," Styles nudged the man closest to the door, "what's your name?"

"Fuck you, bitch!" Came the reply, and a chorus of snickers and laughs burst out through the row of handcuffed criminals.

"That's nice," Styles said condescendingly, "you kiss your momma with that mouth?"

A few "oohs" and "ahhs" from the crowd. Styles bent down and pulled the man up by his shoulders.

"That's Earnest Holloway," Hancock said to Styles, "member of the Uptown Boys."

Styles moved in closer to Holloway and said very loudly for all to hear, "It's little pieces of shit like you that have turned this goddamned city into the shithole that it is!" Styles pushed the man by his shoulders and said, "Move it!"

"Hey!" The man called out scornfully, "Check out Shorty-Pimp!"

Howls of laughter filled the small room, even from the cops. "Shorty-Pimp!" Styles could hear one of Holloway's compatriots echo. Styles kicked the second transport suspect lightly on the leg. "Let's go, chief!"

"Okay, Shorty!" Came the crooked smile reply. As Styles marched the two out the door, Styles wondered about the implications of his newest nickname.

"102 to headquarters," Styles spoke into his shoulder mic as he walked out the glass double doors of 40 Henry Street, also known as the City Jail.

"102."

"102, I'm 10-8, suspects incarcerated."

"10-4, 102, zero four forty-four hours."

Styles looked across to his police car and saw that a certain red-headed dispatcher was bundled up against the night air, leaning against his vehicle. He sucked in his stomach and puffed out his chest and walked briskly over to her.

"Jesus, Adam," she smiled, "take a breath." She held her arms open. He rushed into them, embracing her as if it were their last moments together.

"Mmmm…" she said. "That was nice." Her face glowed in the dark, early morning.

"What are you doing out here?" Styles asked taking in her scent. She smelled heavenly.

"Smoke break," she said.

Puzzled, Styles replied, "But, you don't smoke."

"Oh, really?" She purred and pressed her lips against his. She was so hot against his skin, her kiss warmed him all over. She pulled back. "See?"

Styles was speechless. He was truly in love with this beautiful woman, yet he felt truly awful about what he was doing to his marriage. To his wife. "I see," was all he could manage.

"Well," Mackenzie said, "smoke break's over." She hugged him tightly again. "I just wanted to see you and tell you how madly in love I am with you."

Styles looked into her hypnotic eyes. "I love you too," he heard himself saying. She gave him a quick peck on the check and trotted off, back up the stairs toward the front door of Police Headquarters.

Styles took his keys from his duty belt and reached out to unlock the driver's door. He noticed the writing as he opened the door. Someone had written—in permanent black ink—under the window and above the lock:

Shorty Pimp

He had to laugh.

CHAPTER 9

January 17, 2232 Hours

Dreqel and Kermit were crouched down behind the Quickie Mart at 900 South Sycamore Street. There was a single light bulb mounted over the rear exit door that illuminated the two as they whispered their plan.

"Alright, listen up, K-Dawg," Dre started. "You go in and scope out the joint, walk around all the aisles-make sure we ain't got no one in the back, or no shit like that, okay?"

Kermit nodded.

"They, I'll be out at the payphone out front, see-when you go in and buy like a pack of gum, or some shit, see?"

Kermit nodded.

"Good, then when you think we're all clear-you flash me the sign when you're at the register. Got it?"

Kermit nodded.

"You remember the sign?"

Kermit nodded and put his fingers up to the brim of his ball cap and twisted it to the side.

"That's good!"

Kermit nodded.

"What's up with you, K-Dawg? You fucked up?"

"I'm just sayin', man, I still don't think this is a good idea." The night before, Kermit had come up with the idea of robbing the USA Finance Company on Crater Road. Kermit's thinking was that people were always coming and going, making their second mortgage and car loan payments-usually in cash-and each desk had a cash drawer. There were no video cameras that he could see, and unlike robbing a bank, there would be no F.B.I. involvement. Also, Kermit knew that these convenience stores had very limited cash available, as they were always dropping the money into the safe whenever their drawers reached fifty bucks or so. And the dumbass clerks did not have the combination and could not open the safe. Plus there were cameras. Christ-there was a giant television screen when you walked in the door that showed you that you were on camera! But that was okay, because in Dre's big plan, Dre would be wearing a mask.

Dre was holding the mask as he continued to give instructions. It was one of those popular Halloween masks of a ghost face that was screaming. Dre was finishing the briefing.

"Now when I get the loot, I'll meet up with you back at your house, got it?" Kermit nodded.

"You just stay behind, pretend to be a good witness-wait for the cops and all-and just act dumb."

Kermit nodded. With this plan, it wouldn't be acting.

Soon Yee had been working at the Quickie Mart since six-thirty that morning. She was more than tired, she was exhausted. Patrice, the young girl who was supposed to work the evening shift, had called in sick. And since the store was a family business, and no other family member was around tonight, Soon Yee was elected to stay late.

She had just finished balancing her drawer when she noticed the skinny white kid lurking around the comic books. She noticed him because in this neighborhood any white kid stood out. She went back to her work, keeping one eye on him and his baggy jeans.

The kid had picked up a pack of gum and ambled around to the counter. He placed the gum on the glass shelf that showcased the scratch off lottery tickets. Soon Yee punched in buttons on the beat up cash register and held out her hand.

"Ninety-two cents, please," she said.

Kermit reached into his pocket with his left hand and with his right, turned the brim of his cap to the side. He pulled out a crumpled up one dollar bill. Before the clerk could take the money, a very surreal image flashed from the corner of her eye.

A ghost in a dark sports team jacket burst through the door, wielding a very large gun. Soon Yee focused on the gun.

"Gimmie all yo' money, bitch!" The ghost said.

Soon Yee was frozen. She knew the procedure for armed robbery-she did work in a convenience store, after all-but the mixture of scary mask and big gun was too much for her. She stood rooted, immobilized.

BOOM! A thunderous noise echoed throughout the store as the ghost fired a shot into the ceiling. Particle board rained down from the gaping hole in the tile.

"I said, give me the money, bitch!" The ghost repeated.

"Hey, yo, man!" Kermit said, his acting abilities stretched to their limits. "No one wants any trouble here!" Kermit held his hands up, feigning surrender.

Dre, hidden behind his mask, walked over to Kermit and back-handed him across the mouth. Kermit fell to the ground in one lump. He hadn't seen that coming and Dre definitely did not go over that in the briefing.

Dre hopped the counter and shoved Soon Yee aside hard. He pushed at keys on the register until he finally hit the right one that opened the cash drawer. As if suddenly awakened, Soon Yee began to scream.

"Shut the fuck up, bitch!" Another shot rang out, this one barely missing the woman on the floor by inches. It did have the desired effect of shutting her up. Dre stuffed bills into his pockets, letting checks and change fall free. He pulled the till out of the register, found the larger bills, the 50's the 100's, and shoved them in his pants. Kermit just looked at him in shock, wondering if he'd get hit again.

"You!" Dre pointed the gun at Kermit. Kermit was not expecting this either. "Lay down. On the mother-fucking ground! Now, bitch!" Kermit sprawled out, hands at his side. "Don't you fucking look at me!" Dre leaned in and touched the hot barrel of the gun to Kermit's head. "Don't do nothin' stupid, bitch!" and then lightly slapped Kermit with the metal. Dre ran out of the store and into the night.

Styles had just turned onto Westover Avenue from his Brandon Avenue home in the Walnut Hill section of the City when the alert tone sounded.

BEEEEEEEEEEEEEEEEEEEEEEEEEP!!!!!!! "301, 302, 10-90/10-30 from the Quickie Mart, 900 South Sycamore Street. We have store management on landline who advises 10-30 just occurred. Suspect described as a bravo-mike wearing a ghost mask...all dark clothing...no further. 301, 302 acknowledge."

"301, I copy from Pin Oaks if you've got someone closer!" Officer Sam Grier stated. The Pin Oaks apartment complex was in the city's east end, near the city limits.

"302, I copy from Headquarters," Officer Sharon Taylor advised.

"6907, break!" Styles said into his radio as he had just made the turn from Westover to North Boulevard, and was now on Sycamore Street. "Headquarters, be advised, I'm about five seconds from being 10-6 at the Quickie Mart." Dispatch could hear Styles gun his engine.

"10-4, 6907."

"6905-show me 10-6 as well!" It was Lee Kole. He lived a few blocks away from Styles and must have heard the call on his way into work too. "Direct to 6907, I'm at the store if you want to 10-76 for the suspect."

Styles replied, "10-4. Headquarters, show me 10-76 in the area of 900 South Sycamore Street." Styles had advised dispatch that he would now be canvassing the area for anyone matching the description.

Kole had pulled up into the Chinese restaurant parking lot beside the Quickie Mart with his lights off. He had exited his car with his pistol drawn and hugged the side of the building as he approached and peered into the large glass windows.

Inside the store, Lee began to take inventory of the situation. He saw the two people immediately. With his hand on his weapon he called out, "Police! Is everybody okay?"

Kermit looked up and shouted, "He was gonna kill us, man! He was crazy!"

Then Soon Yee began an incoherent rant in both English as well as Korean. She was hysterical. Kole tried to calm her down.

"Ma'am, it's alright, now…please, take a deep breath." Kole looked over to Kermit, a flash of recognition in his eyes. He also saw that his eye was swollen and the boy was going to have a pretty good shiner before the night was over. "What's your name, man?"

"K-Daw…uh, Kermit." He said, correcting himself for the officer. "Kermit Epstein".

"Well, hang around, Kermit," Kole said, "I'm sure some folks are going to have a lot of questions for you." He keyed his microphone. "6905 to Headquarters, the building is secured, suspect is 10-8. I'm 10-6 with the victims…direct to 6907—you got anything?"

Styles answered, "That's a negative, there's no one on the streets. I've got nothing. Maybe we can get a K-9 up here for a track."

"10-4," Kole responded, "Headquarters, do we have any K-9's available tonight?"

Before dispatch could answer, Officer Stephen "Buddy" Bland's voice came over the radio, "Where you at Lee, I just marked on."

"We're up at 900 South, Buddy, you got Bandit with you?"

"That's 10-4; I'm en-route to you now from HQ."

"100-Bravo," Sergeant Fisk's low voice came across.

"100-Bravo," the dispatcher replied.

"100-Bravo, are there no 300 units working tonight?" Fisk was referring to the evening, or 300 shift officer who were already working and were originally sent to the call.

"That's 10-4, 100-Bravo, 301 and 302 are responding."

"10-4," Fisk stated calmly. "Then, have my officers clear up and report to roll call 10-18."

The dispatcher knew better than to argue with the 100 watch commander. "6905, 6907, 10-19 for roll call, per 100-Bravo."

Kole answered first, and with not just a little agitation in his voice. "10-4, headquarters, you mind if we remain until units arrive? The victims are a little shaken up here."

Before dispatch could answer, Fisk was back on the air. "6905, that's 10-4. You stand by for 301 and 302. 6907, you 10-19."

Styles, who had just pulled up into the parking lot of the Quickie Mart, keyed his mic, "10-4." He then promptly parked his vehicle and went into the store to assist his friend.

"What've we got?" Styles asked Kole, who was still trying to calm down the clerk.

"Well, according to this lady here, a guy wearing one of those scary, horror movie ghost-face masks comes in here and pulls a .40 cal. Then he-"

"Wait," Styles held up his hand, "*She* said it was a .40 cal?" He was obviously skeptical of this lady's ability to identity the model of handgun a robbery suspect used.

"Yeah, she was very clear about it…described it perfectly; color, size, everything."

"Well, she does work in a convenience store," Styles said.

"There's more," Kole continued. "She said that when the suspect pointed the gun at her, she could see something on the barrel." Kole paused. "Some kind of writing and a lot of scratches."

"Are you thinking what I'm thinking?" Styles asked cautiously.

"You better believe I am." Kole replied, "But we'll have to wait for Tommy and the boys at the lab to compare the slugs."

Styles moved in closer and slid his eyes toward Kermit. "What's *his* story?"

"Dunno. Wrong place, wrong time, it seems."

"Uh, huh…" Styles looked down at the counter. "I've got to get to roll call before Fisk has a fit." Kole nodded. Just before Styles left, he turned to Kole, "Hey Lee," he called back. Kole lifted his head. "Just make sure 301 and 302 ask our friend over there why he's buying gum at eleven o'clock at night."

CHAPTER 10

◆

January 18, 0034 Hours

Styles was draining his first cup of coffee for the night. It was going to be a long night. After getting his ass chewed out by his sergeant for having the audacity to assist in a robbery *before* reporting for duty, and not being able to get his regular free cup of coffee at the Quickie Mart, Styles was not in a good mood.

"102, 103." The radio came to life. Styles reached for his microphone to answer the call. "102, Virginia Avenue and High Pearl Street."

"103, 900 block of Hinton." It was Gary Michaels.

"102, 103, respond to 319 South Crater Road, three–one–nine South Crater Road. Be at the entrance to the Blandford Cemetery. 10-25 with the security guard at the main gate in reference to unknown 10-15."

"102, I copy, 10-76."

"103, I copy-any further as to the nature of the 10-15?"

Dispatch keyed her microphone and laughter could be heard in the background from other communications operators. "10-4, 102, 103, 10-5."

Both cops switched their radios over to channel two.

"On two, headquarters."

More laughs. "10-4, 102, 103, be advised, security guard called in report of…report of seeing…people wearing sheets, lighting candles on the headstones…carrying goats." The transmission ended abruptly.

Michaels replied, "10-9, Headquarters, did you say people running around with sheets, candles and *goats*? In the cemetery?"

"That's 10-4, 103."

Styles, knowing just how superstitious his friend was, keyed the mic, and in an effort to lighten the mood, requested, "Any description of the goats, Headquarters?"

More laughs. "That's negative, 102."

Sergeant Fisk came across channel two, "10-91," letting everyone know that that was enough foolishness on the radio.

Blandford Cemetery was one of the most historical sites along the east coast. On the grounds of the cemetery itself stood the Blandford Church. The 18th century parish church was restored in 1901 as a memorial to the Southern soldiers who died during the Civil War. Its Tiffany stained glass windows were still studied and revered by tourists and scholars alike. The weathered tombstones of Blandford Cemetery dated back to the early 1700's, and were surrounded by ornamental ironwork. Some 30,000 Confederate soldiers were buried there and attracted visitors year round. At night, the entire area took on a somber, almost reverent-certainly spooky-look.

When Styles arrived at the main gate, he saw not ghosts or goats, but something equally odd. "102, I'm 10-6 at Blandford," he said into his radio. The security guard was waiting for him, outside the gates, with his car running. The guard was a very large man, maybe 6'2" and close to 300 pounds. By contrast, his car was a tiny Ford Fiesta. Although the man was black, his face was almost white. He was shaking. Something had visibly frightened this man.

Styles pulled up next to him. "What's up, Chief?" He said in his affable manner.

The man came right up to Styles's window. He pulled off his metal security-officer badge and pushed it toward Styles. Styles took it.

"They do not pay me enough to put up with this shit, man!" The name tag on his barrel chest read "TIM JENKINS".

"Now calm down, Tim. Just tell me what's going on." Styles tried his best negotiator's voice.

"Calm down hell!" The man's eyes became as big as saucers as he began to retell the story. "There I am, right? Right in the middle of a goddamned cemetery. I already don't like this job...I hate it when I gots to work the club-but a *cemetery*? What the fuck?!?"

"Okay, okay-cemeteries suck-I get it...but what happened here tonight?" Styles asked as he climbed out of his car.

"Well, like I was sayin', I was right here," the guard pointed to the large iron gates to the historic cemetery. "And I was reading my magazine. They got us out here 'cause of all the vandalism recently, you know?" Styles nodded. "Damn kids knocking over tombstones, spray painting walls and shit-just stupid! Well, I heard this strange noise...sounded kinda like crying or moaning." Styles nodded for him to go on.

"So, I get in my car, and drive around, you know-looking for something-anything. I got me one of those big spotlights just like you have," Jenkins said, putting a big hand on Styles's side spotlight. "Only mine plugs into my cigarette lighter."

"Uh, huh." Styles said, shining his own flashlight out into the darkness beyond.

"Well, there I am, driving around, real slow-like, and shining my light around so I can spot anything unusual-and let me tell you, this place is full of unusual things-when all of a sudden, I see them!"

"What did you see?"

"All them ghosts!"

"And by ghosts, you mean people in sheets?"

"Well, they sure ain't the Klan!"

"What else did you see?" Styles prodded, looking through the iron bars of the gate into the cemetery.

"Well, I seen them ghosts, but I also saw other folks in robes, black robes, and they had the animals."

"Goats?"

"Goats, sheep, I don't know what else. I just know that it's after midnight, I'm all alone in this giant graveyard and I'm not gonna take $6.50 an hour to play Scooby-Doo with a bunch of Satan-worshiping fools! They don't even give me a gun!" Jenkins slapped his leather belt where a holster would have hung.

"Listen, Tim," Styles began, "I understand you're upset..." As Styles was talking, the guard walked back to his car and got in. The driver's side sunk down as he started the engine. "Please, Tim, I'm going to need you if we're-"

Styles was cut off, "Goodbye Mr. Policeman, tell my boss that I'll mail him the rest of the uniform. I'm gonna go work at Happy Burger!" With that, the big man in the small car drove off into the night.

Styles stood there looking down at the security badge the man had handed him as Michaels pulled up into the narrow driveway. "What's up?" He asked of Styles.

"See that little Ford coming out as you were coming in?"

"Yeah, the one with the man cramped behind the wheel?"

"That's the one. It seems our friendly neighborhood security guard was scared shitless by a couple of kids running around in robes with farm animals."

"Adam," Michaels said very seriously, "you know I don't like this shit!"

"What, shit?" Styles played. "Going into the cemetery after dark, looking for those practicing all sorts of witchcraft?" He placed his fingers up around his head like devil horns.

"Cut it out, Adam. Listen, we'll go in, take a quick look and if we don't find anything-we're outta here. Got it?"

"Sure, sure, big boy-sheesh! I'd forgotten what a 'fraidy-cat you were!" Styles headed back to his car when the two cops heard a blood-curdling scream.

"That's it!" Michaels shouted, "I'm outta here!"

"No, wait! Goddamn it, Gary-what if someone's in trouble? Let's go!" Styles jumped back into his car and floored it through the gates. He could see by the trailing headlights that Michaels was reluctantly following behind.

Once inside the actual cemetery, the gravel roads twisted and turned among a forest of gnarled trees and weathered headstones of all shapes and sizes. Styles had his window down and his spotlights on, looking for anything. The lights bounced off stone and marble statues, shrines and mausoleums, then in a blur, he saw something. A cloaked figure, rushing past him. Styles slammed on the brakes and tried to find a place to turn around, but the path was too slim and there were too many headstones.

He looked behind him and saw that Gary had seen it too and had managed to stop his car, leap from it and chokehold the running man with his left arm. Styles stopped his car and ran over to the two. Michaels now had the suspect face down. The person had a hood over his head. When Gary yanked him up by his collar, the hood fell backward, revealing a young boy with unruly hair and now broken glasses.

"Look, Adam-it's Harry Potter!"

Styles had to laugh. "What the hell are you doing here?" He asked the kid.

"It's none of your business-this is public land!" The boy said defiantly.

Michaels slapped him on the head lightly from behind. "Hey, wizard! Read the signs posted everywhere-cemetery closes at dark!" The boy remained silent.

Styles shined his light over to Gary's hands. "Gary-look at your fingers!" Michaels looked down; they were covered in red paint.

"What the fuck?" He grabbed the young man and spun him around. He then took the boy's hands out. They too were covered in red paint. "Okay, Harry, where've you been painting tonight?" The boy said nothing.

"Okay, smartass," Michaels continued as he pulled out his handcuffs, "you're under arrest!"

"On what charge?" The boy now spoke.

"How 'bout pissing me off?" Michaels spat back as he locked the cuffs on the boy's wrists. "And take this stupid Jedi robe off!" Michaels began pulling at the wool cloak.

"Hey, be careful! This thing is expensive!"

"Like I give a shit!"

Styles walked away from the two and let his light fall over the area. About fifty feet from where they were he saw it. Painted onto a section of stone wall on the eastern side of where they were the words:

Beware the Blood Doll

A few feet from the wall was a dog tied to a tree with a rope around his neck where a collar should have been. "Son of a bitch…" Styles whispered out loud. "Hey, Gary, bring that kid down here."

When Michaels and the kid arrived, Styles turned to the kid and asked, "What's your name?"

"I don't have to tell you anything!"

"Did he have anything on him?" Styles asked Michaels.

"I've only searched his robe so far. Found a mini can of spray paint and this," Michaels held up an intricately carved, small blade knife. "Nice, huh?"

Styles shined the light onto the dog, "Uh, huh…and there's your goat. Whose dog is that?"

"I'm not saying anything to you."

Michaels let his hand dig into the kid's back pocket. He fished out a thin, leather wallet. "Mr. Adrian Picardat, 113 Marshall Street…age 19."

"Jackpot!" Styles chimed in.

"Why jackpot?" Picardat asked.

"Because," Styles ruefully smiled, "that means as an adult, I can take you directly to jail, and not have to worry about waiting for a juvenile intake officer!" Styles pointed over to the spray-painted wall. "What the hell's the Blood Doll?"

Picardat remained quiet.

"That's okay," Styles said. "We've got him on felony counts of vandalism, trespassing, cruelty to animals...anything else I'm forgetting?"

"Wait, wait..." Picardat began to talk. "It was just a joke. We were just fooling around."

"Who is we, pussnuts?" Michaels asked. "Where are your buddies?"

"Just some friends; they all took off when the fat guard came by."

"Well, you're gonna give us the names of your friends or you're gonna take the rap for every act of vandalism that's taken place here in the last five months!" Styles said. This seemed to sink in.

"Okay, okay, I'll tell you..."

Styles turned to Michaels. "Can you contact animal control?" He pointed to the dog. "Have them meet us up here or at the shelter? I'm gonna take the Prince of Darkness here down to the station."

"Oh, sure!" Michaels gave a voice of false offense. "I tackle 'em, *you* get the credit!"

"Well, do you want to spend the next two hours filling out paperwork and talking to dumbass's parents?" Styles countered.

"Good point. I'll take Fido down to the shelter."

When Styles had finished with Picardat, he had cleared up six vandalisms and forwarded the names and addresses of four other suspects to Property Crimes. Picardat had written a five page confession/manifesto detailing how he and his "Coven of Apprentices" had desecrated the graves of half a dozen Civil War soldiers. A rambling diatribe of half-baked witchcraft rituals combined with some quasi-satanic cult practices was the end result. No other reason than bored kids who wanted to feel important. Apparently tonight they were to graduate to animal sacrifices. Picardat said that this practice would bring them closer to their powers.

After Styles had secured the confession as well as the warrants for vandalism, trespassing and cruelty to animals, he left the jail and saw what was becoming a familiar sight: Mackenzie Kyle leaning on his squad car.

"Another smoke break?" Styles asked as he pushed up against her and leaned in for a quick kiss.

"Nope." She walked around to the passenger side of his car.

"Then what?"

"Open the door and you'll find out."

"Uh...just in case you haven't noticed, I'm on duty...?"

"Oh, I've noticed." She pointed to the dispatcher patch on her own uniform. "Me too. Have you marked out from the jail yet?"

"No, I was about to."

"Well, why don't you wait about ten minutes. I'm taking an early lunch." She scooted over next to him as far as she could with all of the boxes and switches and other cop stuff in his front seat. "Drive, mister."

"Where to, Miss Daisy?" Styles said in a false chauffeur's voice.

"River Street. Under the bridge. Way under."

Styles drove a block around the Jail toward the city limits. He took a left behind the old Farmer's Market and followed the dark road until they were under the Martin Luther King, Jr. Memorial Bridge. The old bridge was near the even older train station that had been abandoned for several decades. Styles backed his car up as far as it could go under the bridge's furthermost abutment. Mackenzie was halfway undressed before Styles had the car in park.

"Mac, this is crazy—we can't just-" Styles began to protest, but was silenced immediately by two soft fingers.

"Shhh...lean your seat back..." Mackenzie purred.

"It doesn't go back," Styles laughed and knocked on the plexiglass shield, "see this cage?"

She kicked off her shoes and slid out of her blue uniform pants. She climbed over the center console of sirens and radios. She lodged herself onto his lap. She could feel him growing underneath.

"Mac..." he again stuttered.

"Shhh...again came the reply.

Styles could feel her fiddle with his zipper and release the pressure he was feeling with a tug. He slid easily into her. For a moment nothing else in the world existed. Nothing else mattered.

CHAPTER 11

♦

January 18, 0904 Hours

Police Chief Stanley Wayne Kyle was sipping absent-mindedly from his FBI Academy coffee cup while he went through the morning's mail. Sitting in his third floor executive office, Kyle felt pretty good. He stole a glance outside the floor-to-ceiling windows over a beautiful-if not freezing-day in the Cockade City.

Reports, bills, budget requests, and more reports were all stacked up neatly by his secretary Bobbi Hargrove. He took another sip. Then, he came across a letter with the official city seal in gold leaf. *From the Desk of the City Manager,* it started.

Oh, what now? Kyle wondered. As he read, he saw that the City Manager, Richard Covil, had written him a memo apparently in response to a new initiative he had begun in reference to officer rotation. A few months earlier, Kyle had been at a conference for Chiefs of Police and had heard a lot of discussion about shift burnout. This was when a cop had worked the same shift so long, his or her performance suffered. By contrast, those departments who regularly rotated shift assignments seemed to keep higher retention numbers as well as experienced an increase in overall morale.

Kyle had decided that, beginning next month, each shift would begin a three-month rotation to the next shift. The midnight officers on the 100 shift would rotate to the daylight shift. The daylight shift or 200 officers would go to the evening shift, and the evening or 300-watch would rotate to the midnight shift. After their three-month rotation was complete, they'd rotate again. This was to allow each officer to experience more of the city and its various changes in climate with changes in hours.

Although the majority of officers seemed to agree with and even anticipate the change, there was a lot of grumbling from the more veteran cops. Those officers who had ten or more years and had fought long and hard to get their daylight shift assignment were not so eager to go to evenings and midnight work. Apparently those senior officers had made their feelings known to the City Manager.

Richard Covil, as City Manager, liked to run the Police Department more as a department store. Its officers were clerks and the public-both offenders and law-abiding citizens-were the customers. The Chief of Police was the manager, but Covil, of course served as the President. If the clerks had convinced the president that its customers wanted one thing, in this case, shift assignments to remain the same, then Covil would listen to those few malcontents for policy direction. Kyle continued to read on.

∾

TO: Chief Stanley W. Kyle
Chief of Police
FROM: Richard B. Covil
City Manager
SUBJECT: Patrol Officer Rotation & Shift Assignments

Stan,

It is with this letter that I am advising you to discontinue any plan of changing the current patrol officer shift rotation.

I have spoken to several officers who have voiced their concerns to me in reference to your current plans to rotate each shift.

I feel this would have a detrimental effect on the department in general and the City specifically.

Please contact me if you have any further questions or concerns.

*Well, I'll be a son-of-a-bitch...*Kyle thought to himself. *Who does this prick think he is?* Kyle remembered when Covil was first hired. He demanded that, as City Manager, he be given a police badge and gun along with a radio. Since he was over the Chief of Police, it only seemed fair that he have the same toys. Kyle thought back to the time that Covil's office was broken into and his badge, gun and radio were stolen. In addition to causing great embarrassment to Covil, it allowed all of his men to act silly on the radio and blame the real thief.

"Bobbi!" Kyle shouted for his secretary.

"Yes, Stan?"

"Come in here, please, I have a job for you."

CHAPTER 12

◆

January 18, 1604 Hours

Adam Styles was dreaming. It was a reoccurring dream. Sometimes the circumstances and situations of the dream were different, but each time, the major theme was the same: a feeling of powerlessness.

In the dream, Styles was chasing after the bad guy, fighting with the bad guy, getting ready to shoot the bad guy. Every time he drew his weapon, the gun wouldn't fire. Sometimes in the dream, the bullet would simply fall out and roll to the ground. In the dream, it felt tangible and that fear, that feeling of helplessness, translated over into real life. It haunted Styles in situations where he had to pull his gun. No matter how many times he did any maintenance, cleaned his weapon, or trained at the firing range, Styles was always aware of the dream.

In his dream, Styles felt pressure on his left leg. He looked down, there was nothing there. Then, in his dream, he heard the voice of his wife. Suddenly the world of his dream melted away and the world of his bedroom came into focus.

"Adam, wake up." Susan Styles patted her husband on the leg.

Styles rubbed his eyes, "What's wrong, what's the matter?" He saw that his wife was in her nursing uniform. Her Petersburg General Hospital nametag reflected the light of the bedside table. "What time is it?"

"It's a little after four." Susan sat down on the bed beside him. "Adam, we need to talk."

Styles's heart sunk. Already racked by guilt, he knew that in the history of relationships, nothing good ever came from the words, "we need to talk."

Styles sat up and propped his pillow behind him. "Okay, Susan, let's talk." He looked at her. "You first."

Susan Styles looked down at her hands and began. "Adam, I love you very much."

"I love you too, Susan, what—"

"Please, don't interrupt." She put her hands out without looking up. "Just let me finish."

Styles nodded.

"As I was saying, I love you very much. You have been a good husband." She swallowed hard. "I know…I know that we've had our problems lately. But, I just have to know that we're both still committed to," she seemed to be searching for the right words, "well, that we're both still committed to us."

Styles said nothing, he just stared at the woman across from him. The woman he fell in love with so many years ago. Styles looked at the woman who had stood beside him for so long and felt sick to his soul. He had betrayed this angel.

"So," Susan stood up and straightened her uniform, "what do you say?"

"What do I say?"

"Yeah, what do you say? Are you still committed to us?" Her voice was calm, cool, but Styles could read between the lines. What his wife was really saying was "I know all about your girlfriend, and I want to know who it's going to be: her or me?"

"Yes." Styles stood up beside her and took her hand. "Yes, I am committed to us. I love you very much, too." They hugged each other. When she pulled away, Styles caught something in her eyes. The look echoed her voice. But, for whatever reason, she nodded and simply said, "Good."

"I'm on my way into work," she picked up her car keys off the nightstand, "there's some leftover chicken in the fridge." She then kissed him lightly on the cheek and headed for the front door.

Styles watched his wife drive away and at that moment, he knew what he had to do.

CHAPTER 13

♦

January 18, 1927 Hours

Styles was off duty. But, as with most police officers, Styles always needed extra cash. So, Styles had settled himself into a corner booth at the Big 'n Hearty Burger located at the corner of Washington and Union Streets. Big 'n Hearty had been hiring off duty cops for about two years now, ever since a particularly nasty robbery took place and one of their managers had their brains splattered against the fry bin. Styles couldn't help but look at the fryer each time he came into the place. Tonight, his special duty shift was from 1900–2300 when they closed.

Styles had checked in promptly at 1900 hours with the manager and had grabbed a soda and the day's newspaper. He was just finishing the editorial pages when he noticed, out of the corner of his eye, a very disheveled older man standing by the counter. Not really in line, but just standing there. He seemed harmless enough, maybe homeless. He didn't look like he weighed a hundred pounds soaking wet. He was muttering to himself. Styles went back to his newspaper.

On the other side of the restaurant, two more patrons came in. Drequel and Kermit were bickering fiercely about Kermit's black eye.

"All I'm sayin', man, is you could've told me about smacking me like that!"

"Man, shut the fuck up!" Dre whispered through clenched teeth. "I had to make it look real, didn't I? Besides-if I had told you I was gonna hit you-would you have let me?"

"Well, sure, if you had told me." Kermit was pouting.

"Look here, K-Dawg, if I had told you, you would have been expecting it. So when it came, it wouldn't look real!" Dre dug into his pockets and pulled out a wad of bills. "Now, get me a burger, bitch! I'm gonna go to take a piss."

Kermit scowled and headed up toward the counter. He saw the old man.

"Hey, pops? You gonna order?"

The man didn't acknowledge Kermit. In fact, he didn't seem to acknowledge that he was even in a restaurant. Kermit stepped around him and approached the first cashier.

The man began walking toward the center of the establishment and started to verbalize out loud.

"They're everywhere. They're here and they're not going away." The man grumbled. This caught Styles's attention. He put his paper down.

The man saw Styles. He saw his uniform. *Like a moth to a flame*, Styles thought.

"Hey, Officer! Officer!" the old man shouted.

"Yes, sir. I'm right here, you don't need to yell."

The man lowered his voice to a conspiratorial tone. "I'm sorry, Officer." He came even closer to Styles, who was seated with his back against the wall. "It's just that they're everywhere...I *know* you've seen them!"

"Seen who, sir? What are you talking about?"

"You, know...*them*." The man pointed up to the ceiling. Styles followed his gaze. Just when Styles was about to write the old man off as another loon, a flash of glistening metal swooshed out from under the man's jacket. Suddenly, Styles found himself less than three inches away from a very shiny, very sharp, hunting knife. The kind that survivalists use, with the serrated blade on one side, and the sleek, smooth blade on the other.

Stupid, stupid, stupid! Styles silently cursed himself. How could he have allowed himself to let his officer safety become so lax? Here he was, pinned up against the wall, the blade of a madman's knife so close he could smell the leather handle.

"They've been here a while, Officer-I know you've seen them!"

Styles thought quick. "Of course, I've seen them...why do you think I'm *here*?" This seemed to confuse the old man. Styles matched his conspiratorial tone and winked, "I got a tip. They love the Big 'n Hearty burger...that's why I'm here. *Waiting* for them!"

Across the room, Kermit had just turned and was now watching the drama unfold. Dre was coming out of the bathroom.

"No mother-fucking paper towels in there, yo…" Kermit tapped him on the shoulder.

"What?" Dre demanded, but then got quiet when he saw what Kermit was looking at. Over in the corner, a cop was being held up at knifepoint. This was going to be good.

"Hey, man," Kermit said to Dre, "that cop was there at the Quickie Mart!"

"No shit!" Dre said.

"No shit, we gotta get outta here!"

"Why? He don't remember you! And he damn sure don't know me!" Dre stood unmoving, fascinated by the prospect of seeing a police officer get cut right in front of his eyes.

"Let's watch this shit!"

A million thoughts were racing through Styles's mind as he tried to figure out a way to end this peacefully. The restaurant had people in it, but not that many. He saw that only a few seemed to have noticed what was going on. If he could get the man to put down his knife-even a little-he could draw his weapon and…and what? Shoot into a crowd of people? At this distance, it was guaranteed that he would hit him, but it was probably just as sure that the bullet would go right through the skinny old man and into a customer. He'd have to play this one very carefully.

"Anyway," Styles pressed on, "I've got a secret weapon."

The old man's face lit up, "Really? What's that?"

"Well, it's a special Krypton bullet…" Styles motioned with his hands up. "Can you, uh, put that knife down?"

The old man's face carried a wounded look, as if he took great offense at the thought the nice policeman was scared of him. He immediately pulled the knife away from Styles's face.

Just as immediately, Styles pulled his pistol and leveled it at the old man's head.

"Shit! Did you see that?!?" Dre punched Kermit in the shoulder.

"Ow! Yeah, I see it!"

The old man seemed even more confused now; not sure of just what was going on. Why was the nice policeman with a secret weapon to stop them now pointing his gun at him?

"Listen up, sir. I need you to drop the knife right now," Styles said, his voice becoming authoritative.

The man did not move.

"Now, sir!" Styles cocked back the hammer on his .40 caliber Smith & Wesson.

The man simply let go of the knife and it clattered to the floor.

"Back away from the knife, sir," Styles commanded.

The man took a few stumbled steps backwards. "You're one of them, aren't you?"

Styles re-holstered his weapon, kicked the long knife aside and took the man by the arm toward the counter. "No, sir, I'm not. But I think you'd better come with me." Styles produced a pair of handcuffs from his duty belt and gently but firmly placed them on the man. "Let's go, sir." He nodded to the manager who began clapping as did those patrons who had witnessed the entire exchange.

Two people not clapping were Kermit and Drequel.

CHAPTER 14

♦

January 18, 2214 Hours

"Man, I'd a shot that mother-fucker so fast he'd never even see it comin'!" Dre was retelling the story of what had happened at the Big 'n Hearty Burger to their makeshift crew. Kermit was in the middle of the group, backing up Dre.

"Yeah, man," Kermit answered, "that bitch would have been toast!"

"'Cept, I tell ya'll this-" Dre kept talking, taking a sip from the community forty ounce bottle of malt liquor the five boys were passing around, "If I'd been that old man, I'd a cut that pig from ear to ear!"

"True dat!" One of the group added to the conversation.

"True dat!" Another echoed.

The motley group had assembled at one of their favorite corner hangouts, the intersection of Halifax Street and Saint Matthew Street. Here, they could style and profile in their black jackets and maybe even sling a little dope if anyone was holding. And since they were right next to the Easy Go gas station, they could buy a soda or snack and use the bathroom. What else could a street thug want?

"Man, Dre," one of the group asked, "What would you have done if that guy *had* cut that cop?"

"Shit!" Dre answered and rolled his eyes. "You mean after I finished laughing my ass off?" This solicited a few snickers among the friends. "I'd watch that mother-fucker, and make sure he didn't think he could cut nobody else…" Dre pulled back his jacked and pulled up his matching sweatshirt. The butt of the 9 mm. was poking out from his baggy jeans. The small crowd grew instantly silent.

"Then, if he looked like he was gonna do something stupid-like come at me-I'd put a cap in his ass my damn self!" He took an even bigger swig from the bottle. "Don't know why that stupid cop didn't blast that bitch in the first place!"

Kermit made a face that told Dre to cover up the gun. He had warned Dre not to show or tell anyone about the piece. But here he was, getting drunk and running his mouth. Finally, someone said, "Damn, Dre...where'd you get that gat?"

Dre pulled it out for all to see. The stainless steel shining under the street lights. "What, this?" Dre held it up to his face as if it were a lover. "It's been in my family for years!" He laughed at his own joke. Everyone else just looked at the gun. When he saw no one else was laughing, he squeezed off three rounds. BAM! BAM! BAM!

Everyone scattered like mice except Kermit. "Dre!" He scolded. "What the fuck are you doing?" Kermit pulled Dre's arm down and tried to cover the gun with his coat. "Are you trying to get arrested?"

Dre, taking great umbrage, recoiled. "You better step off, bitch!" He pushed Kermit away, the gun still in his hand, steam rising from the barrel.

"You're drunk!" Kermit shouted and turned to run away.

"Yeah, run, bitch!" Dre shouted back and fired off a few more rounds into the night, laughing maniacally.

CHAPTER 15

♦

January 19, 2314 Hours

Sergeant Fisk had been listening to the nightly roll call proceedings as Assistant Squad Leader Cecil Perkins finished up all of the routine topics. After all the BOLs and notices were over, Perkins asked if there was any new business. Fisk stood with a stack of papers in his hands.

"Okay, listen up, people," Fisk began. "As you know, a few months ago, we received notice that we would all begin to rotate shift assignments very soon." Grunts, groans, and cheers were sprinkled around the conference table where the men and women of the 100-Bravo shift were gathered.

"I have here in my hands a questionnaire from the Chief. I need you to fill it out and return it to me by 0300 hours." Fisk began passing out the forms. "They are pretty self-explanatory, just check the boxes and answer the questions."

Officer Susan Denton began reading the form. "Sarge?" She asked, "It seems these questions are asking us our preferences and opinions as to why and how we should rotate. Hasn't that decision already been made?"

"Denton, I know what you know. I only take orders. And tonight, my orders are to pass out these questionnaires and get them back from you."

"Sounds like the third floor doesn't know what it's doing!" Gary Michaels stated flatly.

"Well, I hear that soon, this whole idea of rotating is going out the window!" Officer Frank Certo said. "I hear that some of the war horses on the day-shift went to the City Manager and bitched about having to move!"

"No way!" Denton said.

"Way!" Certo responded. "These guys said they had worked long and hard to get where they were and no one was going to make them work nights!"

"Ain't that some shit!" Officer Eddie Jefferson commented.

"Typical," Michaels added.

"Okay, okay, break up the editorial, people." Fisk interrupted. "Let's hit the streets!"

As the cops were getting up from their seats, Cecil Perkins blocked their exit at the rear door. He held his right hand up; in his left hand, he held a piece of paper.

"What's up, Cecil?" Fisk demanded.

"Bad news." Perkins let his head fall. "Just got word from Petersburg General. About fifteen minutes ago, S.A.N.E. Nurse Ashley Granger succumbed to her wounds...she's dead." Perkins paused a moment to let the news sink in. Then, "For those of you who knew Ashley, there will be an announcement tomorrow as to where and when a memorial service will be held."

"Son of a bitch..." Styles said, his own head bowed.

Perkins raised the piece of paper and his right hand again. "Also, this just came in off the teletype...I didn't get it before roll call. There's been another rape. This time in Dinwiddie. Same M.O. as Ashley's. The victim's up at Petersburg General right now. It looks like she'll pull through, but according to Dinwiddie, it's the same guy."

Silence fell over all of the cops assembled. One of their comrades had fallen and the monster who took her was still on the loose. Still hunting.

CHAPTER 16

◆

January 20, 0159 Hours

"102, 112." The voice of the dispatcher broke the silence of a relatively quiet night.

Styles picked up his microphone. "102, High Street."

"112, Upper Appomattox," Lee Kole responded.

"102, 112, respond 934 Farmer Street, nine-three-four Farmer Street. 10-16 involving husband and wife. Called in by neighbor. No further."

Styles logged the call on his activity sheet and keyed his mic. "102, copy and en route."

"112, same."

Styles made a quick left from High Street onto a side alley that lead up to Washington Street. He had crossed over to Farmer from Halifax. The air was colder now and the weatherman threatened snow. Before he could make it to Washington, the alert tone sounded.

BEEEEEEEEEEEEEEEEEEEEP!!!!! "102, 112, be advised that 10-16 has become 10-83. Caller advised husband has 10-83ed his wife."

"102, copy—responding code-three." Styles hit his overhead blue lights and sirens as he floored the gas.

"112, copy." Styles could hear Kole's sirens engage as well.

Like a shark, Styles maneuvered through the city streets with determination and purpose. The report was of a woman who had been stabbed; her life could depend on whether he or Lee Kole got there in time. This pressed on his mind as his foot continued to press on the accelerator.

He came upon an intersection where he had the red light. He slowed just enough to see there was no traffic. Bureau rules dictated that he come to a complete stop at all intersections even when running code-three, however Styles blew through the light at forty miles per hour. He could hear his car's engine protest as he gunned for more speed. He was just a few blocks away from the scene.

"102 direct to 112, what's your twenty?" Styles did not want to enter the house alone, but with a life at stake, he would.

"112, I'm coming to you, I'm about one minute away."

"102, copy. Headquarters, show me 10-6 on Farmer."

"10-4, 102," Dispatch confirmed. "All units, channel one is 10-3 for 10-83, 934 Farmer Street. All units, channel one is 10-3 until further notice." Headquarters had cleared all radio traffic for Styles and Kole. All other traffic was now routed to Channel two.

"112 direct to 102, stand by, I'll be there in just a moment!" Kole advised.

Styles was getting out of his car. Lights still flashing, he put his PR-24 baton into its holder on his duty belt and unsnapped his pistol. As he approached the front porch, Kole's patrol car hopped the curb and Lee jumped out, pistol in hand.

The two cops nodded to each other as Styles banged on the front door. "Police!" He challenged, "Open up!"

"Help me!" Came a desperate cry from inside. The voice was distinctly male. "Get in here, goddamn it!"

Styles tried the door. It was unlocked. The two cops rushed forward and immediately were stopped just feet inside by an arc of flowing blood.

Lying on an overturned loveseat was a man grasping his upper leg. Bright red spewed out in a measured rhythm, in sync with the beating of his heart. An arm's length away was a woman. She was still holding the large carving knife.

"Holy shit, she's hit an artery!" Kole shouted. Another rush of blood flooded into the living room and onto the floor.

"Femoral artery to be exact," Styles agreed as he reached for the tiny pouch that held his rubber gloves. "Didn't this call come in as the *female* who was stabbed?"

"Crazy bitch gonna kill me!" The wounded man said, pointing to the knife-wielding woman.

Lee Kole wasn't listening to the man's claims; he had his weapon trained on the person who could do the most damage. "Drop the knife, ma'am!" He stated forcefully. "Do it now!"

If the woman heard, she didn't let on. She screamed, "Lying, cheating, mother-fucker!" When it looked like she was about to draw back for another swing, Kole issued a final ultimatum.

"Ma'am! I will shoot you right now!" He let those words sink in, then, "Drop the knife!"

The woman turned now to the officers in her home, as if just suddenly realizing that they were here. She also focused on Kole's pistol. She dropped the knife and lunged at the man on the floor.

"Lying, cheating-ass, mother-fucker!" Her attack grew more vicious as she began slapping and kicking the downed man.

Styles didn't know what was worse, trying to break up a domestic fight or dodging the spurts of blood that kept shooting out at him in different directions as the man moved for cover. He pulled out his PR-24 baton and used it as a brace to separate the two opponents.

"Ma'am", he tried. "Please, stop it…its over!"

"That bastard's been sleeping with my cousin!"

"Fuck you, you crazy bitch!" Now the man tried to smack the woman through Styles.

"Hey!" Styles protested, then turned to Kole, "Cuff 'em both!"

Kole moved in and took the bleeding man over to the opposite side of the living room. Blood splashed onto his uniform and covered his bare hands. He turned the man over and handcuffed him while Styles secured the woman.

"102 to Headquarters, we're 10-95 two times, tell rescue that it's safe for them to enter!" Styles called in on his shoulder mic. He looked down to his own uniform. Blood spilled onto his shirt and pants leg. "Great," he said, nodding to Kole.

Two members of the Southside Virginia Emergency Crew came barreling in through the open door. Both large, burly men with the requisite buzz cut flat-tops.

"I told you!" The first paramedic said to the second one to enter the house.

"Yep, you called it!"

Styles looked to Kole. Nothing. Then, "What're you guys talking about?"

"You guys don't know these two?"

Styles and Kole shook their heads as they got the two up and moved them toward the door. Kole pointed to the stabbing victim and said, "Hey folks, can we get some direct pressure on this leg here?" Right on cue the blood shot up and arced across the room.

"Whoa!" The second paramedic said, "Glad you guys are gloved!" Then, he looked down at Kole and saw that he was not wearing any gloves. "Shit, man-be careful!"

Before he could elaborate, the woman jumped from Styles's grip and landed right onto her male companion. She began biting him about the neck and shoulders.

"Oww!" The man cried out, "Get her off me!"

Kole instinctively reached for the woman's head with his forearm and pulled her back with a headlock move. The woman then turned her attention on Kole. She bit down hard into his arm through his uniform and sunk her teeth deep.

"Arughhh!" Kole winced with the pain and with one mighty blow, punched the woman backwards three feet. She fell to the ground, knocked out like a light. Kole rubbed his arm.

"Oh, shit, man," The first paramedic said as he came over to him. "What my buddy was trying to tell you was that this is Mavis and Ritchie Barker!"

Styles and Kole held a blank look on their faces.

The second paramedic took over. "We're always up here on some call or another! These two are always going at it! Usually they're drunk and passed out by nine!" The big man leaned over to look at Kole's arm. "They're high-five!"

Then it sunk in. High-five or HI-V. The street slang for someone who was HIV positive.

"Oh, fuck!" Styles said, looking at Kole and then to Kole's arm. "How bad is it?" He asked his friend.

Quietly, Kole stated. "Bad enough. Broke the skin."

"Shit, man, let's get you to the hospital. They got stuff for that, but we gotta get you there now!"

Kole brushed him aside. "I'll drive myself." Turning to Styles he said, "Adam, call 100-B. Let him know what's going on. Get someone up here to transport."

"Yeah, man, no problem," Styles said and reached again for his microphone. "You going up there now?" He called out, but Kole was already out the door. Styles heard Kole's car break traction as it squealed away down Farmer Street.

CHAPTER 17

♦

January 20, 0235 Hours

The snow had begun to fall when Styles pulled up in the lot of Petersburg General Hospital's rear emergency lot. He could feel the flakes melt on his cheeks as he opened the police car's trunk and took out a change of clothes. Styles's uniform had blood spatter on both his shirt and pants. It was a good thing that he always kept a set of utilities in an old foot locker. The locker held extra paperwork, ammo, road flares, a first aid kit, and a variety of other police-related specialty items.

He took out an extra large plastic evidence bag in which to discard his dirty uniform, and carrying the work clothes, walked through the ambulance doors and into the police officer's lounge. At this time of night, it was deserted. He quickly changed clothes and admired himself in the full length mirror hung on the back of the door. Styles always thought the utilities looked like a mechanic's uniform. The only difference was the patches. He could have gone home for a fresh set of digs, but he didn't want to wake up his wife. The thought of his wife, sleeping in their bed, rocked him with pangs of guilt.

After stashing the soiled pants and shirt into the evidence bag, Styles walked briskly out into the main E.R. to look for his friend.

The E.R. was unusually slow for a midnight shift and Styles saw Kole being attended to by two nurses.

"Where's the doc?" Styles asked as he approached. "Hey, Shelly," he nodded to the ladies, "Kelly." The girls smiled back.

"He's gone to get some test results or some shit," Kole answered in a grim voice and with an even grimmer face. Styles looked to the faces of the nurses for some help. Shelly studied the floor, Kelly just shook her head.

"So," Styles continued, "What's the prognosis?" He kept his tone light, breezy.

"You mean do they know if I've got AIDS?" Kole snapped back. "Isn't that what you mean?" The nurses took their cue to leave and headed back to the nurses station located in the middle of the giant E.R.

Styles leaned in closer, looking at Kole's bandaged arm. "Look, man," Styles started softly, "I know this sucks, I really do, but—"

"Do you, Adam? Really? Because I don't think you do!" The look of anger was red on Kole's face. "I've been a cop for over seven years. I've been in hundreds of fights, been shot at, I've been cut, and…" Kole paused, as if not quite sure where he was going with this, "…and, well, I know that sometimes we deal with drones who have all kinds of shit-AIDS, TB, you know? We always take precautions, we always glove."

Styles interrupted him, "But, Lee, we can't always be take precautions in some of the situations we get into. Sometimes we're put into things and we fly by the seat of our pants. We try, but we can't be prepared for everything every time!" Styles knew his friend was aware of this as well, but felt he needed to hear it again.

Kole remained silent, looking down at his arm. "The doctor said he was going to start me off on that cocktail right away."

"Cocktail?"

"Yeah, you know-the combination of all the AIDS drugs out there, all at once? The cocktail."

"Oh, yeah." Styles did remember hearing about the so-called AIDS cocktail from his wife. "How long will you have to take it?"

"Every fucking day. They'll test me every week at first for the virus, then once a month, and then every six months after that for about a year or so. Just to make sure." All expression had left Kole's face.

"102." Styles's radio sprang to life. Styles reached for his microphone. "102-Petersburg Hospital, 10-6 changing uniforms."

"102, when you're 10-8, need this unit to respond to 1113 Liberty Street, one-one-one-three Liberty. 10-60."

Styles looked at his friend.

"Go on, man, there's nothing you can do here. I'll get with you later," Kole said.

Styles nodded and spoke into his radio. "10-4, Headquarters; show me 10-8."

CHAPTER 18

♦

January 20, 0240 Hours

The rapist lay on his bed, naked and aroused. Lying across his groin was a colorful cloth lanyard with a Petersburg General Hospital ID tag attached. As he stroked himself, he glanced down at the yellow, sponge-shaped cartoon character on the blue background. He smiled.

The rapist closed his eyes and held the souvenir closer to him. He held it and remembered the thrill of taking if from her. He remembered the rush as it pulled against her neck and long, brown hair. She didn't even realize he had taken it, she was such a fighter. Well, for a girl. A few slaps and grabs for starters got her going, but the well targeted and powerful blows kept her under control. He was becoming more excited now, wrapping the neck cord around his member.

He turned the ID toward him. ASHLEY GRANGER, RN it said in big yellow letters. PETERSBURG GENERAL HOSPITAL and then in a smaller font: EMERGENCY ROOM STAFF. She really was a fighter. The memories of that night came back to him in a flood of white, hot flashes. He looked again at the ID, at the picture-her picture. That was all it took. He felt the release.

He lay motionless now on his bed, basking in the afterglow of his vivid thoughts. He remained there for a few minutes, then he reached for the dirty towel on the floor beside his bed. He wiped himself and stood.

The rapist walked over to the pile of soiled laundry that his aunt had not yet got around to washing and dug through the pockets of a pair of filthy jeans. The ID card wasn't the only souvenir he took that night.

He fished around in the front of the pants and found what he was looking for, a folded up piece of paper with pictures of little knives and forks printed on it. The paper said:

Who loves to cook?
We're having a Pampered Cook Party!
When? January 22 @ 4:00 pm
Where? Marilyn's House
Please R.S.V.P. before January 16th!

Below the text was a little map, detailing how to get to Marilyn's house in Chesterfield County. The rapist had already driven by. Twice. He liked what he saw. Marilyn was a nurse too.

CHAPTER 19

♦

January 22, 0925 Hours

The Chief of Police sat in the lobby to the City Manager's Office. Stanley Wayne Kyle was not a man accustomed to being kept waiting. But, waiting he had been this date. He had an 8:30 meeting with Richard Covil to discuss the latest on his shift rotation idea. Kyle glanced at his watch and exhaled deeply as he looked out the ornate windows that overlooked downtown from City Hall. This did not escape the attention of Covil's secretary, an older heavyset woman in no mood for the Chief's disgruntlement.

"Excuse me," Kyle asked the woman, "any idea when Dick is going to be ready to see me?" Then, for good measure, he added, "It's been an hour."

The secretary put on her best "I don't give a shit" face, added her phoniest smile and replied, "I don't know, Chief Kyle, he's got a very full schedule today."

"Yes, I know," Kyle stated flatly as he got to his feet. "I'm on it." The Chief of Police walked briskly around the large woman and her large desk toward Covil's private office door.

"Chief, you can't—"

But he did. Kyle entered the City Manager's office and saw that he was on the phone. Noticing the visibly annoyed look on his face, Kyle sat down directly in front of him.

"Well, tell Frank the red will be fine, dear," Covil said into the receiver, wrapping up the call. "I've got to go now, someone's just come into my office. Love you too, bye." He hung up the phone.

"A little rude, don't you think, Stan?" Covil asked.

"No, Dick," Kyle answered, "rude is making me wait an hour to see you when *you* requested this meeting."

Covil did not try to hide his contempt for the man in front of him. "Alright, Stan, I'll get right to the point. Did you get my memo dated seventeen January?"

"I did."

"Good, so now, I can formally document your official insubordination."

"Excuse me?"

"In my letter, I advised you to cease and desist with this shift rotation thing you've come up with. By your own admission you got this directive and yet you have continued to go forward with it."

Kyle held his hands up. "Listen, Dick, first of all, no shifts have been changed, so your directive is still being honored. Secondly—"

Covil cut him off by flipping a piece of paper up from his desk and holding it at arms length so Kyle could see it. "Then, just what the hell is this?"

Kyle could see it was one of the shift rotation surveys he had asked the watch commanders to hand out to their officers. "It should be evident, even to you, Dick, what that is. It's a survey. It's a survey that I distributed so that-once all the data was collected-I could come back to you and advise you of just how many officers were in favor of shift rotation." Kyle paused and took the paper from Covil's hand. "Which is the vast majority, I might add."

Covil stood up and leaned in on his desk. "Stanley, I want you to listen to me very carefully." Covil's voice became just more than a whisper. "I don't give a shit what you think. I didn't ask you to take a goddamned poll. I gave you a direct fucking order and with all due respect, I expect you follow it!" Covil walked over to one of many floor-to-ceiling windows in his office. With a grand, sweeping gesture, he swung his arms up as if to offer himself up to the good people of the city. "I am in touch with this community, Stan. I know what its people want and I know what its officers want and need. I talk to the cops walking the beat, Stan. I know their concerns. I've spoken with those cops who have been here the longest and they have assured and convinced me that mixing up the shifts is the worst possible thing you can do!"

Kyle remained seated. "With all due respect to you, *Dick*, you don't know one damned thing about police work or my officers. You think I don't know who you've been talking to? You think that I'm so out of touch that I don't know that the only cops who are making a stink about this—and running behind the Bureau's back to you—are the same handful of malcontents counting the days until their retirement?" Covil turned to look at the Chief.

Kyle continued, "These are the same complacent humps who, after working a few years, managed to make it to daylight shift, where they became fat and lazy. Home every night. Able to work the precious part time and special duty jobs their evening and midnight shift counterparts can't because of the hours." Covil pulled his chair out and sunk into it. It was Kyle's turn to stand.

Kyle walked over to Covil, continuing his tirade. "Do you even know any of the stats on patrol officer burnout? What working midnights year after year can do to a man? Under my plan, the officers would work no more than six months in each shift rotation. That's just enough time to get the officer and his body acclimated to the new hours and yet not long enough for them to become worn out." Kyle, who was much taller than the City Manager, leaned over the man in his chair and pointed his finger. "Do you even realize the turnover rate we have? The majority of our entire force has been here less than ten years!" Disgusted with Covil, Kyle made a beeline for the door. "That's why I began the study into the shift rotation." Kyle reached for the knob, but did not turn it. "That's why, with the help of the Department of Criminal Justice Services, I came up with a plan of action. That's why I conducted this survey." Kyle flung the paper to the floor. "You may have made the powers that be give you a badge, Dick-but you're no cop!" He opened the door and noticed that five staff members were all huddled next to the large secretary's desk. "Stick to what you know best: raising taxes and running all the businesses out of town!" Kyle slammed the door shut on his way back to police headquarters.

CHAPTER 20

♦

January 22, 1134 Hours

Maymont is a sprawling park in the middle of Richmond, between the James River and the historic Fan section of shops and homes. Half nature preserve with its buffaloes, bears, and goats, and half outdoor retreat with its gardens and rolling hills for hiking and biking, Maymont provides a nice respite from the day-to-day grind of the world. Twenty minutes from Petersburg along Interstate 95, and one can walk paths between exotic birds and pet the horses.

This January morning, snow covered most of the green, but the sidewalks and walking paths were clear. Adam Styles and Mackenzie Kyle walked hand in hand.

"Gee, Adam," Mackenzie said, "a little chilly for a picnic, isn't it?"

Styles smiled, "Well, I just thought it would be a nice place to have a little privacy." He squeezed her hand. He did not look forward to what he had come here to do.

"What? Are you breaking up with me again?" She laughed. She stopped laughing and turned to him when she did not get a response. "Hey!" She said, "I'm kidding."

Styles said nothing.

"*Are* you breaking up with me again?

"Mac, listen," Styles tried to say but was interrupted.

"Oh, shit, Adam!" Mackenzie said, loud enough for other park goers to hear and look their way. She turned and walked toward the parking lot, her breath trailing in the cold air.

"Mackenzie, wait!" Styles called out and caught up with her. He took her gloved hands in his, and she quickly pulled them away. "Mac, you don't understand, there are reasons why—"

"I'm tired of your reasons, Adam. When we're together, everything's fine! No-when we're *fucking*, everything's fine! Then, you go home to that bitch, and suddenly, there are reasons!" She stormed off again, a little faster. "Well, you can take your reasons and you can shove them up your ass!"

"Mac, where are you going?" Styles shouted, "I've got the keys!"

"I'm a big girl, Adam-I think I can find a ride!"

Styles ran past her and stopped in front of her with his arms outstretched. "Mac, I love you, I really do, but—"

"No you don't, Adam, no you don't! You love the idea of you and me. You love the memory of us in junior high. You love fucking me—"

"Mac, *please!*" Styles looked around at the passing joggers and strollers.

"Well, it's true! If you loved me, you'd be with me. You'd hold me at night instead of her. But you want your cake and to be able to eat her too!" Mackenzie bolted around Styles off the walking path and into the snow-covered grass. Styles followed.

"Look, you're right!" Styles pleaded, "Okay, you're right! I'm sorry, I didn't mean for this...*any* of this to happen." He took a deep breath. "But I realized that when it comes to my wife, I just—"

"I get it! Okay, Adam! I fucking get it!" She was screaming now. "I'm just sorry that I ever thought I could come first in your life. I'm just sorry that I ever thought that you could love me again-love me with all of the promises you made me! I really thought you could love me as much as you said you did when we were naked!" She was crying but was determined not to let Styles see it, so she blew her nose into her scarf. "I get it, okay? I was a fool!"

"No, Mac, that's not it...I—" Styles reached for her.

"Goodbye, Adam." She kept walking. "Goodbye!"

Styles stood on the cold hill and watched her leave.

CHAPTER 21

♦

January 22, 2139 Hours

"Man, this is bullshit, K-Dawg!" Dre said to Kermit as they sat in Dre's bedroom again, scheming. Dre had gone through all of the four hundred plus dollars they had stolen in their Quickie-Mart heist. Kermit had managed to net about seventy dollars out of Dre, but he didn't mind. Dre seemed to be in a good mood the next few days, despite his alcohol-fueled rages. Now, Dre had decided, it was time for another job.

"I mean it, this is bullshit!" Dre cried out again. He was unusually pissed off because he just found out that the Halifax Street Market had added armed security guards to its front doors last month. The market was known in Dre's neighborhood as the place to go cash your check, pay your phone or light bill, and every now and then, borrow a little money under the table from old Mr. Burgess, the proprietor. At a modest interest rate, of course.

"I'm telling you, Dre," Kermit spoke up. "We need to lay low for awhile. We hit another place in less than a week, the cops gonna know it the same guy. You!" Kermit walked away from his friend and looked out the bedroom's lone, dirty and broken window. "I've told you before, Dre, these convenience stores are nowhere, man! They're not gonna have more than fifty-sixty dollars on hand. That Quickie-Mart, or the little mom and pop places like the Market are different 'cause they're not national chain stores. But, you go into a place like the Market-before the guards-and someone's bound to recognize you!" Dre lay on the floor with his eyes closed. He was listening, but not liking what his friend was saying.

"What about the Try-N-Save?" Dre grunted.

Kermit looked down at him incredulously. "The Try-N-Save? The grocery store all the way down Crater Road next to J-Mart?"

"Yeah, why not? They open twenty four hours. They got a safe. They cash checks," Dre propped himself up on his elbows, suddenly brought back to life by his own idea. "They even got one of them send-money things!"

"Send-money things?" Kermit asked.

"Yeah, you know, nigga-one of them places you can give 'em money and they can wire it to people and shit!" Dre was literally scratching his head now. "You know what I'm saying-Western Money Gram or something…"

Kermit did know what he was saying. But Kermit also knew it was a stupid idea. "Dre," Kermit started off softly, "that place is huge. It's too big-how you gonna get in and out quickly? And with a mask?"

"Won't wear no mask, fool." Dre was standing now. Pacing. "We go in, ask to see the manager-tell him we got a complaint or something. Then, when he shows up, we bust out with the .40!"

Kermit just stared at Dre.

"What?" Dre demanded.

"We bust out with the .40? Where do we do that, Dre? Right there in front of the cash registers? Maybe in front of the frozen pizzas?" Kermit could see by Dre's expression that he was not happy with his tone. Kermit began talking a little faster. "What I'm saying, man, is there will be too many people there. And what about transportation? We gonna take the bus? Call a cab? How we gonna make our get away?"

Dre had not thought that through. How *would* they get away? Then the idea hit him.

"Hey man, yo mamma's got a car, right?"

Kermit did not like where this was heading. "Uh, sure, Dre, but she ain't gonna drive us out there, wait in the car while we rob the place, and bring us home." Nervous laughter slipped out of his throat.

Dre grabbed Kermit by both shoulders. "We ain't gonna ask yo mamma to drive us." Dre's eyes squinted as if he were about to share an intimate secret. "We gonna take yo mamma's car!"

"No way, Dre. No way!" Kermit protested.

"Whatchu' mean, 'no way', bitch?" Dre shook Kermit hard. "Let's go get that mother fucking car, right mother fucking now!"

"Now?" Kermit snapped free of Dre's grip. "You wanna rob the Try-N-Save…now?" Kermit looked at his watch. "At ten o'clock at night?"

"Sure, nigga-why not?"

Kermit began to stutter. "Well, uh…uh, for starters, my mom would notice the instant we took the car. It's a piece of shit! Nothing but an old Buick! Its got a fucked-up fan belt-makes all kinds of noise when you first start it up. She'd be out of the house in an instant!"

"So," Dre countered, "we'll be long gone by then!"

Kermit couldn't believe he was even having this conversation. "Look, Dre. Enough's enough. It's late. I'm going home." But before Kermit could even make it across the small bedroom, Dre was on him like a linebacker. Dre threw him to the floor and straddled him. Digging into his pants, he pulled out the gun. He shoved it right under Kermit's chin.

"Look, bitch," Dre said with more menace than Kermit could remember, "we gonna get yo mamma's car right fucking now. Do I make myself clear?" Dre cocked the hammer on the pistol back carelessly with his thumb, all the while pressing the barrel hard against Kermit's skin.

Kermit nodded.

CHAPTER 22

♦

January 22, 2333 Hours

"112," Lee Kole spoke into his shoulder mic, "show me 10-6 at the Crater Road Lanes."

"10-4, 112, twenty-three, thirty-three hours." Dispatch called back to him.

Kole pulled up to the front door of the bowling alley and observed the usual Saturday night crowd of bowlers coming and going.

"112, can you 10-9 the description of two suspects..." Kole scanned the group, "or have the complainant step outside."

Dispatch repeated the call, including the description, "112, call came in as a 10-15/10-16 between a whisky mike and two whisky foxtrots. Manager called in to say all parties involved in 10-15. Be advised, suspects will be two whiskey foxtrots, both 10-56, arguing over a..." the abrupt silence took Kole by surprise. Was there new information? Was there a weapon involved? "112, two subjects will be fighting over a pink bowling ball." More silence. When the radio traffic from dispatch resumed, not so muffled laughter could be heard in the background. "112, complainant, Mr. Hopkins will be meeting you at the main entrance."

Kole stepped up to the curb, and saw through the glass front doors what had to be the two white females in question, as they both appeared to be attached to a shiny pink bowling ball. Kole entered the main lobby, and called it in. "112, I've got 'em, show me inside the establishment."

"10-4, 112. 102, do you copy?"

"102, I copy. Direct to 112, I'm at the light at Sycamore and Adams coming to you."

Adam Styles advised headquarters and his friend.

Back inside the bowling alley, Kole saw two women screaming at each other. Each woman had her thumb firmly ensconced in one of the bowling ball's holes. He approached the two women. Both looked to be in their mid-thirties, both blonde, and both were wearing entirely too much make-up and hair spray. Although they were shouting full blast at each other, neither one of them relinquished the orb between them.

"Drop it, you bitch!" The first blonde screamed.

"It's my goddamned ball, you whore!" The other replied.

"Whoa, whoa," Kole stepped in and put his own hands on the ball. This seemed to shock the women into silence. "Ladies, what's going on here?" Kole noticed a man running toward them.

"That's them, officer, that's them!" The running man shouted. "I want them all gone, their boyfriend too!" The man pointed to a group of gangly looking men over by lane fourteen. All of the men turned their backs when they saw the man point.

"He's my goddamned boyfriend, not hers!" The second blonde cried out.

Kole kept his grip on the ball. "Are you Mr. Hopkins?"

"Yep, that's me. I'm the manager. These two been fighting for about the last thirty minutes or so-all over that guy right there!" The man pointed to the men again.

"Gerald!" The man shouted to a long-haired, skinny man with a leather vest over a dirty yellow tee-shirt. "Gerald! Get your ass over here!"

"Sir, please," Kole cautioned, "there are kids and ladies present." This made more than a few folks in the crowd around them laugh. Kole turned his attention to the first blonde. "Ma'am, what's this all about?"

"I'll tell you, officer!" The woman's speech was slurred and Kole could smell the booze from a foot away. "This bitch here's trying to take my ball! *My* boyfriend gave it to me!"

"That's a goddamned lie!" The second blonde spoke up.

"Ladies!" Kole shouted in his best authoritative cop tone. "I'm not going to tell you again about the language.

"It's my ball!"

"It's my ball!"

"Actually, it's my ball." The man Mr. Hopkins called Gerald was walking up to them.

"Care to explain, sir?

Gerald let his eyes fall to the floor as he explained. "Well, you see, uh," Kole could smell alcohol on his breath as well. "Kimmie, here," he pointed to the second blonde, "she's my girl…"

"See, bitch? He loves me!"

"Ma'am!" Kole broke in.

"Sorry."

Gerald continued, "And you see, we meet here on Saturdays to bowl and I bought this here ball for her to use."

"You cheatin' mother fucker!" The first blonde shot back.

Kole shouted over everyone, "Alright! The next person to swear in my presence is going to jail!"

Everyone looked remorseful. Gerald continued, "But, you see…on *Fridays* me and Roberta come in here to bowl."

"You son of a bitch!" Roberta screamed.

"Alright, that's it!" Kole said as he whipped out a pair of cuffs. He pointed to Roberta.

"You're under arrest. Drunk in public. Let's go!" Kole clicked on the cuff to her free hand and swung her around to grab the other. He pried her thumb out of the ball and clicked the other cuff tight. Kimmie clutched the ball to her chest.

"Ha! Slut! You're going down, whore!" Kimmie taunted.

"You too, lady, drop the ball!" Kole pulled out another pair of cuffs from his belt.

"No, you can't!" Kimmie protested, but Kole yanked the pink ball away and tossed it to Gerald.

"Here!" Kole called out. Gerald almost fell over from the catch.

Kole spun Kimmie around, clamped her wrists together, and slapped on the cuffs.

CHAPTER 23

♦

January 22, 2347 Hours

Kermit pulled his mother's 1986 Buick Skyhawk alongside the curb in front of the Try-N-Save. Even though it was almost midnight, the place was still very crowded. The lot was full of cars and customers were coming and going. Kermit peered into the store through the automatic sliding doors and saw that at least three registers were open.

"Okay, man," Kermit turned to his friend, "what's the plan?"

"The plan, K-Dawg," Dre pulled the hood of his black jacket up over his head and pulled the draw strings tight, "is that we go in there and get some mother fucking money!"

Kermit rolled his eyes and covered his head with a gray wool stocking cap. They both put on large, dark sunglasses. "You want me to stay here, keep the car running?"

"The car can run all by itself, nigga!" Dre shot back. "Get your ass in there now!" Dre pulled out the gun and motioned to the door with it.

As soon as the two walked through the main entrance to the store, they were bathed in bright, florescent light. Kermit turned to Dre, "Yo, where's the manager?"

"I don't know, fool!" Dre's head shook left to right. "Let's just start blasting!"

"No, Dre—" Kermit's voice was drowned out by the sound of two gunshots back to back. Screams drowned out anything else.

"Listen up, you mother-fuckers!" Dre shouted out to the cashiers and customers. "We want money and we want it right mother-fucking now!"

CHAPTER 24

♦

January 22, 2352 Hours

Kole had both Roberta and Kimmie by the arm as he led them to his squad car. They were both kicking and screaming, but not loud enough for Kole to miss the alert tone that sounded from his portable radio.

BEEEEEEEEEEEEEEEEEEEEEEEEEEEPPPPPPPPPPPPPP!!!!!!!!!!

"112, 102, any available unit," dispatch relayed, "10-90, 10-30...10-30 in progress thirty-two hundred South Crater Road. Three-two-zero-zero, South Crater-the Try-N-Save. Have manager on land line, reports same is being 10-30ed at this time. Suspect description, one whiskey mike, one bravo mike. Bravo mike has 10-32 and both are still inside at this time."

"Break!" Kole let go of his two female prisoners and grabbed his microphone. "112, to headquarters, I am directly across the street from the Try-N-Save at this time, show me 10-6!"

"10-4, 112. All units, channel one is 10-3 for 10-30 in progress at thirty-two hundred South Crater Road, Try-N-Save. Channel one is 10-3. 102?"

Styles came across the radio, "102, I'm coming up on you from Crater Road at South Boulevard, stand by for me!"

"102, that's 10-4, but I'm approaching on foot. Kill your siren and park next to the J-Mart lawn and garden center!"

"10-4." Styles cut his sirens but not his lights and continued to weave through traffic.

Kole called out to Gerald who was standing with his little group of men, "Hey, come get these two!" Kole bent down and unlocked the cuffs on each of the girls.

"What?" Kimmie shouted, "we're free to go?"

"Yeah, are we un-arrested?" Roberta chimed in.

Kole took off in a sprint toward the supermarket across the street. "Yeah," he shouted back, "get the hell outta here!"

Inside the Try-N-Save, Mark Warren, the night manager, was on the phone in a stockroom near the front end. He had seen the whole thing go down while he was looking for a mop. He had shut the door and called the police. Looking through a crack in the door, he had been giving a play-by-play to the dispatcher.

"Now, the white boy is going from lane to lane with plastic bags, collecting the money from the registers." Dispatch was relaying this information over the air to Kole and Styles.

"The black kid's the only one with a gun it looks like-the white boy hasn't pulled one yet. The black kid's just waving it around and shouting!" Warren reported, his voice excited. "Hurry up, where's the cops?"

"Sir, they're on their way, please just stay calm and stay on the line with me."

Kole was hugging the building as he approached the Try-N-Save, his gun drawn and held low by his side. He could see Styles flying up Crater Road and turning left at Morton Avenue. He held his position, listening to the radio updates. Kole noticed a beat up Buick with the exhaust chugging out of the tailpipe. Still running.

BLAM! Another gunshot rang out.

Kole moved closer to the doors, running on instinct. He inched his way just to the outside of the sliding doors and crouching down, moved his head only a fraction to take a peek inside. He saw the two suspects standing together by register four. True to the manager's word, it appeared as if only one of them was armed. Then he saw something that made his heart lurch. Lying on the floor, next to the register itself, was an older man. He was bundled up tight with a large wool coat, cap and scarf. Kole couldn't tell if he'd been shot or not, but he knew he had no time to guess. He had to take action.

Kole moved in close, still hugging the walls of the interior lobby. He then raised his weapon and took aim at the one suspect with the pistol. He had the shot. He was about to take it when the suspect turned to his partner and began yelling. Then Kole saw it-the suspect was just a kid.

"What the fuck yo mean, why'd I do that?" Dre was yelling. "I shot the mother-fucker to show these bitches we mean business!" Dre pointed the gun at

Kermit's head. "Now, go get the rest of the money before I show *you* I mean business!"

Kole had no other choice, it was now or never. "FREEEEEZE!" Kole commanded, his own pistol trained on Dre.

You could have heard a pin drop. Everyone, customers, the suspects, even Kole it seemed, had stopped everything and remained frozen. Dre's eyes opened wide as he saw the policeman's gun pointed directly at him.

Just as quickly, Dre came back to reality. "Back the fuck up, cop!" He said as he motioned to Kermit with the gun. "I'll shoot this bitch!"

"Yo, yo, Dre, come on, man!" Kermit pleaded.

Outside, Styles had parked his cruiser and made it past the J-Mart on his way toward the Try-N-Save. "102 direct to 112-what's your twenty?"

No answer.

"102 to Headquarters," Styles whispered into his mic, "I'm 10-6 at the Try-N-Save, no sign of 112. I'm heading in."

Styles cautiously made his way to the front door of the Try-N-Save. Like Kole a few moments before, Styles crouched down and stole a look inside. He tried to take it all in, to make sense of what he was seeing. He sank back and keyed his mic.

"102 to headquarters, I am outside of the business, unit 112 is inside and has his weapon on one armed suspect. Suspect has a pistol aimed at a hostage. Stand by for further!"

Kermit felt his pants go warm and wet. He didn't have to look down to see that he had pissed himself. "Holy shit, Dre! Don't do nothing stupid!"

"Yeah, Dre…" Kole snapped back, "don't do nothing stupid."

"Shut the fuck up, bitch!" Dre said to Kermit, "You too, cop!"

"Yo, Officer," Kermit was shaking, "You don't know this fool-he crazy!"

"Fool!?" Dre asked Kermit, "Fool? I'll show you fool!" Dre squeezed off another round. The sound was deafening.

Kole immediately fired off three rounds in quick succession. All three bullets found their target—Drequel Sanders, center mass. As the slugs tore into Dre, they spun him around and off his feet.

Dre, still clutching the pistol, managed to fire off five more shots. Three flew wild, landing in the ceiling and smashing the glass behind Kole. Two, however, found their way to Lee Kole.

Dre went down. Kermit did not. The shot grazed his right ear, but lodged safely in a wooden display shelf full of potato chips.

Styles burst into the store and called out, "Lee, you okay?" He saw Kole was bleeding heavily. He screamed into his radio, "102 to headquarters, 10-100, Officer Down! I repeat, Officer Down!" Styles bent down to help his friend.

"He got me, Adam-he fucking got me!"

Styles ripped open Kole's uniform shirt and revealed his bullet resistant Kevlar vest. Lodged in the right side of the material, Styles saw the slug. It would leave one hell of a bruise, but not life threatening. Where had the other bullet gone? Then he saw it. Just under the bullet he was looking at was a red burned streak of black and red. Where the vest met and fastened at the Velcro straps, blood was running out.

"Hang on, man!" Styles tried to comfort Kole. Styles pulled apart the straps carefully. More blood shot out. Just near the heart. Styles did his best to sound confident. "Shit, Lee, nothing but a flesh wound. You're gonna be fine!" Styles looked up and saw a crowd gathering. "Hang tight, buddy, it's just a knick!" He stood up. "Listen up, folks, please, I need you to stand back and give us some room!" Styles looked over to Kermit. "You okay?"

Before he could answer, Mr. Warren, the night manager ran up to them. "He's one of them, Officer!" Warren shouted out. "Look, there's the money, in the plastic bag!"

"Yo, yo, my brother, I don't know what he be talking 'bout!" Kermit began to walk backwards toward the door. "That guy is whack!"

Styles pulled out a set of handcuffs and grabbed Kermit's wrist hard. "Knock off the Harding Street horse shit, wigger!" Styles clamped one set of the cuffs to Kermit's right hand and the other to a metal pole attached to the cash register.

"Hey man, what the fuck?" Kermit whined, "That dude shot at me and *I'm* the one being handcuffed?" Styles gave Kermit a steely stare and walked toward Dre. With his left foot, Styles stepped on Dre's hand-still holding the gun.

Styles looked down and saw that Dre was not breathing. He bent over and took the gun from Dre's lifeless grip. He quickly saw the inscription of his own department on the side, despite an attempt to file it off. *I'll be damned, Joe's gun*, Styles thought. The crowd behind him was getting loud and starting to move toward the front.

"Please!" Styles commanded, "Ladies and gentleman, I need everyone to stay back!" Styles could hear the sound of approaching sirens. He keyed his mic. "102, unit 112 is down and one suspect is 10-7. Other suspect is 10-95. ETA on rescue?" He went back to sit down beside his friend.

"102, be advised rescue ETA one minute." Dispatch advised. Styles did not acknowledge.

Styles leaned over Kole; Kole's eyes were open, but they were no longer seeing anything. "Lee?" Styles tried. *Oh, God...no!*

CHAPTER 25

♦

January 23, 0025 Hours

The rapist hid behind a set of large boxwoods in Marilyn's front yard. The shrubs had grown quite thick over the years, and even without the snow to pad the empty spaces between branches, they provided excellent concealment.

He waited until he saw the all of the lights go off in her home before he lifted his head out of the hedges. He peered in through the frosted window and into the dark home. Long shadows were cast by a tiny, fluttering nightlight she kept plugged into a kitchen wall. The rapist made a mental note of the light. He'd have to get rid of that.

He closed his eyes and imagined all of the things he was going to do to her. But not tonight. Tonight was reconnaissance only. He inched around the side of the house until he settled in under Marilyn's bedroom window. From there, he dared a peek inside.

He could see her there, her head resting on two fluffy pillows. He made a note of the pillows as well.

CHAPTER 26

◆

January 23, 0120 Hours

Styles sat in a deserted hallway of the Petersburg General Hospital just outside the emergency room with his head slumped over and resting on his knees. It had been one hell of a month. In the past two weeks, one of his fellow officers had been shot. A friend and damn fine nurse had been brutally raped and murdered. He had his heart broken. And today, one of his closest friends had been killed.

Somewhere, one floor below where Styles sat, was the body of Lee Kole. Styles had been there when the E.R. doctors had officially declared Kole dead. It wasn't necessary, as Styles had seen the last bit of life leave him on the dirty floor of that godforsaken grocery store. Styles saw them pull the sheet over his body and wheel him toward the elevator bound for the morgue on the first floor.

The questions were endless. How did this happen? Who was that kid? Was he the one who shot Joe? Was it his fault that Lee was dead? What if it was him? Who would take care of Susan? What about Lee's family?

That last question lingered. Kole's parents lived in Prince George, just over the city limits. He only had one sibling, Beth, his sister. Outside in the lobby, Kole's mom, dad, sister, and assorted aunts and uncles—friends and well wishers—were gathered in grief. He couldn't face them.

Styles knew that he should be out there, somehow trying to console them, but he could barely keep himself together right now. He had called Gary Michaels and got his machine. He didn't leave a message. Michaels had the night off and God only knew where he was. Styles just hoped he could reach him before he heard the news on the radio or television. Kole and Michaels were even closer than Styles and Kole. Kole had actually lived with Michaels while they were going through the academy with Styles. Michaels was going to be crushed. It was a good thing, Styles thought, that the kid had been killed, because once Gary found out what happened, he would have surely killed the boy himself.

Styles tried in vain to push the image of his friend lying in his own blood, eyes going vacant, staring up at the tiled ceiling of the Try-N-Save. He tried to block the memory of the E.M.T.s working on Kole, running IVs, recording vital signs (or lack thereof), the lights, the sirens; they were all a horrible blur to Styles. He could feel the tears leaking out from his eyes. Styles tried to hold them back, but it was futile. Then, the dam burst and he sat there in the secluded space of a hallway that lead to a service elevator crying to himself, letting the tears and the snot fall out of him and onto the floor. He kept his head down and wept.

Styles could not hear the soft voice beside him as he wailed out in pain into his folded arms. It was not until he felt the gentle touch on his shoulder that he noticed he was no longer alone. He looked to his left and saw a pair of women's feet. He recognized the shoes.

"Susan?" He didn't look up.

"Hey, Adam," she said quietly as she squatted down beside him. "How are you holding up?"

"How did you know about—" his words trailed off.

"Are you kidding? The phone's been ringing off the hook." She put her arm around him. "Your dad, my dad, Gary," she offered her husband a tissue.

"Gary?" His head snapped up, tears still wet on his face. "So he knows?"

"Yeah, he and Sherri are in Virginia Beach. He heard it on the news."

"Virginia Beach?" Styles blew his nose loudly and wiped his face. "Does he know it's January?"

Susan smiled. "I guess they wanted to get away. He said he was packing up and on the way." She glanced at her watch. "That was about thirty minutes ago, so he should be here in about an hour or so."

Styles blew his nose again.

"Anyway, once I got the call from your dad, I knew you'd be here, so here I am." She rubbed his back and could feel his Kevlar vest under his midnight blue uniform.

He looked at her for the first time. "Thank you. I'm sorry you had to see me like this, I really—"

"Shh," Susan Styles put her finger up to her lips. "None of that tonight, okay? I don't need any of your macho cop shop bullshit."

This made Styles smile for the first time. "I know, honey, it's just that the only time I think you've ever seen me cry is when my grandmother died."

"And now, your best friend is dead. Killed right in front of you." She leaned in and held him. She could feel the dampness of his shirt. "I think it's alright if you let it out."

Styles tried to take a deep breath, but halfway through, he choked up again and the tears and the moans would not stop. Susan pulled him closer and held him tighter.

They held onto each other like they were the only people in the world.

CHAPTER 27

♦

January 25, 1216 Hours

The funeral of a police officer is an awesome sight to behold. The pomp and ceremony are truly awe-inspiring. Row after row of uniformed guardians with their somber, solemn faces. Family, friends and well-wishers huddled together in a sea of black. Television crews and newspaper reporters recording the powerful images for their audiences.

To some, an ignorant minority; the death of a police officer is no big deal. Part of the job. Line of duty and all that. But, if they stopped and thought about it, they would realize that it is a very big deal indeed. Especially the murder of a cop. Think about it, if some punk isn't afraid of a specially trained and well-armed law enforcement officer, with years of experience in working the streets, why would he (or she) be afraid of the average citizen?

Styles looked around as almost every cop in the state who wasn't on duty was gathered around him in dress uniform. All had black bands taut across their badges.

He noticed that some of the surrounding jurisdictions had ornate, double-breasted suit coats, draped with lanyards and braiding. Styles turned to the section of the cemetery where the Petersburg Police had gathered. The Petersburg Bureau of Police did not have a specific dress uniform, so all of the officers and dispatchers were dressed in their class-A, long sleeve shirts. The officers were also wearing their official police hats. It always struck Styles odd to see a Petersburg cop in his "bus driver" hat because they were seldom worn. On the streets, when chasing down a drug suspect or fighting with a drunk hooker, headgear had a tendency to fall off.

The memorial service before they arrived at the graveside was fitting. The Prince George church that hosted it barely had enough room for family and friends. Most of the officers had to wait outside. Although a member, Kole hadn't been to church since he was seventeen.

It was cold and overcast on a dreary January morning. The weatherman threatened freezing rain, maybe mixed with snow. So far, the clouds had held.

Styles was standing at attention next to Gary Michaels. This had been especially hard on Michaels. He was off on the night it happened, and somehow had processed that fact into a feeling of responsibility. Through the filter of guilt, Michaels had convinced himself that if only he had been on duty, maybe there was something he could have done.

Styles and Michaels had been pall-bearers. They carried their friend's flag-draped coffin out of the church and into the cold. Once at the cemetery, they carried him to the grave. It was one of the toughest things they'd ever had to do.

Styles and Michaels were no strangers to death, not even the death of one of their own. Between the two, they had been to more than their fair share of cop funerals. No matter what the cause of death, car accident, heart attack, even suicide, they covered their badges with black nylon and put on their bus driver hats. Although they had known most of the cops whose funerals they had attended, some were strangers. They were cops from other jurisdictions, state troopers. They didn't know them, but they were cops.

Styles stood rigid next to Michaels as they listened to the preacher recite words meant to comfort loved ones. Styles only heard the tone of voice; he had tuned out the world, instead focusing on the memories of his friend and the future of his own life.

Styles was in the first row of officers lined up to pay their final respects to Lee Kole. He scanned the crowd and found the eyes of his wife. Susan gave him her best sympathetic glance. Styles gave a tight smile in response. His eyes continued to wander. They fell on the group of non-sworn employees of the Petersburg Bureau of Police. He went from dispatchers to secretaries until his gaze found Mackenzie. As soon as she caught his look, she turned away. It was a cold, hard day for Adam Styles.

The service ended and a mass of mourners drained away in a trickle of lingering uniforms and tears.

Epilogue—Part One

♦

January 26, 0842 Hours

Stanley Kyle sat down at his desk and sipped his first cup of coffee of the day. It would also be his last. He flipped through the morning mail, tossing out solicitations for money and stacking up invitations and speaking engagement requests. Then, he saw it. The letter was addressed simply,

S.W. Kyle

And had the return address of

OFFICE OF THE CITY MANAGER

In the upper left hand corner.

Christ! Kyle thought as he ripped open the cream colored enveloped and read its contents.

ⱷ

TO: Chief Stanley W. Kyle
FROM: Richard B. Covil
City Manager
SUBJECT: Employment Termination

Mr. Kyle,

It is with this letter that I am officially terminating your employment with the City of Petersburg as its Chief of Police.

Effective immediately, you will return your gun and badge, as well as all uniforms and insignia to the Property Office. You will also turn in your city vehicle to Fleet Maintenance.

Should you have any further questions or concerns, please direct them in writing to the Office of Human Resources.

Please vacate your offices by COB this date.

That son-of-a-bitch! Kyle thought as he felt himself balling up the paper in his hands. *That son-of-a-bitch!*

Epilogue—Part Two

♦

January 26, 0023 Hours

Marilyn Carter pulled up to the curb in front of her home in Chesterfield County. She was tired and hungry. What a night. She had just finished her shift at Petersburg General Hospital and was now looking forward to food and sleep. In that order.

She made her way up the concrete walkway to her front door. As she pulled out her keys from her heavy purse, she noticed that her porch light was out. She always left it on, as she worked the evening shift and usually arrived home after midnight. She didn't notice the splintered wood along the doorframe as she put her key inside the lock and turned it.

Marilyn walked inside her living room and noticed with some alarm just how dark it was inside. She was sure she left the kitchen light on as she always did. She flicked the switch on the wall closest to her. Nothing. Suddenly a light flashed on from her right. Her bedroom.

She stepped over to the coffee table, where her phone was. The receiver was off the hook, its cord severed. She heard movement. From the dark hallway she could see a dark figure emerge from the shadows. Marilyn ran for the kitchen. She slammed her fist into the stove light switch and a dim yellow haze filled the room just in time to illuminate the stranger in front of her.

Standing in the doorway to the kitchen was a man, naked except for a shower cap and a pair of dishwashing gloves. The man held a large carving knife in his hand. He walked slowly toward her, taking in every nuance of her face.

Marilyn did not say a word as the rapist inched closer. Their eyes were locked on one another. He smiled. Her face remained emotionless. He was saying something to her now, but she wasn't listening. She was terrified.

The rapist was within a few feet of her. She could smell the sweat and body odor of her attacker. She did not say a word as she pulled out her .38, five-shot, snub-nosed revolver and fired five rounds directly into the rapist's chest.

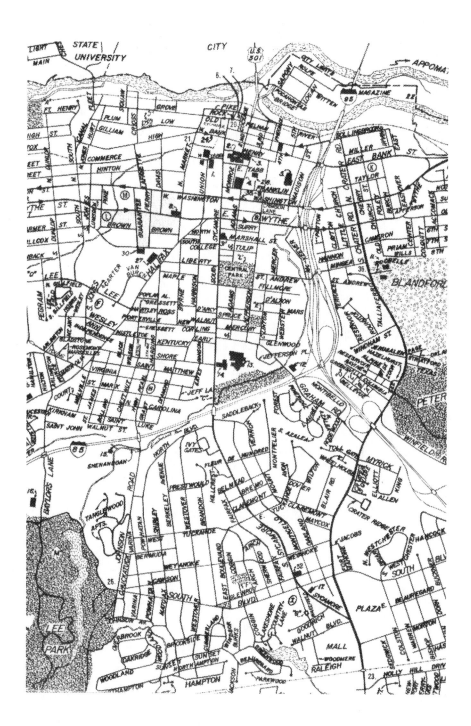

Petersburg Bureau of Police Ten Codes

♦

10-1   Unable to Copy

10-2   Transmission Good

10-3   Stop Transmitting, All Channels—EMERGENCY TRAFFIC ONLY

10-4   Okay or Affirmative

10-5   Relay or Direct to_____

10-6   On Scene or Busy at Location

10-7   Out of Service

10-8   Back In Service/Clear from Assignment

10-9   Repeat

10-10   Meal Break

10-11   Investigation

10-12   Official/Visitor Present

10-13   Restroom Break

10-14   Prowler

10-15   Disturbance

10-16   Domestic Disturbance

10-17   Domestic Violence

10-18   Complete Assignment Quickly/Respond Quickly

10-19	Report to Headquarters
10-20	Location
10-21	Call by Phone
10-22	Disregard
10-25	Meet with_____
10-26	Picking Up or Dropping Off Package/Item
10-27	Drivers License Information
10-28	Vehicle Registration Information
10-29	Warrant/Wanted Check (Local, State, or National)
10-30	Armed Robbery
10-32	Person with a Gun
10-33	EMERGENCY—Officer Needs Help
10-34	Panhandling
10-35	Fight in Progress
10-36	Time Request
10-37	Suspicious Person, Situation, or Vehicle
10-38	Shots Fired
10-39	Wanted/Stolen Confirmed
10-40	Stopping Traffic Violator
10-41	Beginning Tour of Duty
10-42	Ending Tour of Duty
10-43	Walk Through
10-45	Dead Animal at_____
10-46	Assist Stranded Motorist/Disabled Vehicle at_____
10-48	Premises Insecure at_____
10-49	Adult Abuse
10-50	Accident (Property Damage, Personal Injury, Fatality)

10-51   Wrecker

10-55   Intoxicated Driver

10-56   Intoxication person

10-57   Hit and run (pd-pi-f)

10-58   Working traffic

10-59   Escort or convoy

10-60   Burglary

10-63   Prepare to Copy

10-64   Canvassing the Area

10-65   Send Backup Unit CODE-THREE

10-67   Radar in Use

10-70   10-70M Murder, 10-70R Rape, 10-70S Suicide

10-74   Negative

10-76   En route to

10-77   Dead Person

10-80   Pursuit, 10-80F Foot Pursuit, 10-80V Vehicle Pursuit

10-81   Drugs/Narcotics Violation

10-82   Person Shot

10-83   Person Cut/Stabbed

10-84   Assault, No Weapon Involved

10-85   Larceny/Theft

10-86   Stolen Vehicle

10-87   Shoplifting

10-88   Purse Snatching/Mugging

10-89   Alarm Out of Service

10-90   Alarm sounding (10-90/10-60, 10-90/10-30)

10-91   Unnecessary Use of Radio Traffic

10-92	Change Radio Channel to_____
10-95	Prisoner/Suspect in Custody
10-96	Mental subject
10-97	Juvenile
10-98	Exercise
10-99	Bomb Threat
10-100	Police Officer Injured/Officer Down

About the Author

◆

Steve Armstrong is a former police negotiator with the Petersburg (Virginia) Bureau of Police, and is the author of two previous Cockade City novels, a collection of editorial cartoons and a children's book. In 2003, Steve and his father, Major (Retired) Edward Armstrong, published the first of a new series of military thrillers set against the backdrop of the Vietnam War.

Steve now lives in Richmond with his wife, daughter, and three dogs. Visit him at his website—**www.stevearmstrongonline.com**

0-595-31712-X